# THE TRIBALIST

*A novel by Louis Marano*

ISBN: 1503289796
ISBN 13: 9781503289796
Library of Congress Control Number: 2014920985
CreateSpace Independent Publishing Platform
North Charleston, South Carolina

# PART ONE

# CHAPTER ONE

Israel – April, 2000

Dahlia Tamir removed her sunglasses and squinted against the glare. Although she was in uniform and had been to the prison many times, it was best to establish one's identity as quickly as possible.

Unseen eyes continued their scrutiny as the outer gate opened. She entered the antechamber, dropped her cell phone, keys and coins into the tray, and walked through the scanner.

The senior guard was always pleased, if a little bemused, to see the attractive lieutenant colonel. In three years' army service, now long past, he had emerged a staff sergeant. But although he and Dahlia both were in their early forties, more than rank separated him from this comely brunette, who – while formal and correct with the prison staff – saved her smiles for the Arab security prisoners. Another one of those arrogant north Tel Aviv *Feinschmeckers*, he thought, who imagine only they and their sort are clever enough to find the secret of placating Israel's sworn enemies.

"Good afternoon, colonel."

"Good afternoon."

He knew the routine, and he had been told that today Lieutenant Colonel Tamir would want to speak with Ahmed Asfour. He escorted Dahlia through the prison complex, reaching a room that had been set up for interviews. He nodded to Yossi, a young guard standing in the hall, who hurried off and soon reappeared with the prisoner.

"Mr. Asfour, your psychologist is here," Yossi said in English with a heavy Israeli accent.

Yossi withered under Dahlia's reproachful stare. He exited, took station outside the room, and kept watch through a window in the door. Dahlia's face softened as she greeted Asfour.

"*As salam 'alaykom,*" she said.

"*Wa 'alaykom as salam,*" he replied.

She gestured toward a folding table, and Asfour sat down in one of the molded plastic chairs. Dahlia assumed a seat across from him, facing the door. She glanced up at Yossi, watchful through the plexiglass.

"Do you still want to practice your English?"

"Yes, please!"

"Have you heard from your family?"

"A letter. With pictures!"

Asfour took an envelope from his pocket and handed Dahlia snapshots of a woman in a headscarf, two boys, and a girl.

"Lovely. You must be very proud of them."

"Yes, of course."

"And they're proud of you, aren't they?"

"Everything I do, I do for them."

Dahlia paused, thoughtful.

"My research is almost complete," she said. "Soon I'll write my final report. Then I'll be retiring from the army."

Asfour looked stricken.

"This place, what it does," he said, as if in explanation. Seconds elapsed. "It's pleasant to talk with a woman like you, modestly dressed. One summer I worked at an ice cream stand on the beach in Tel Aviv. It was shameful how the women exposed themselves there."

"Maybe we can do something for you."

"I would never collaborate!"

"I wasn't suggesting that." Dahlia took some papers from a file folder and reviewed them. "Let's go over a few things. The two others who were involved with you in recruiting the suicide bomber --"

"—were hunted down and killed by Shabak."

Dahlia looked up from her papers and into his eyes. "The nephew of a friend was on that bus."

"I'm sorry for your friend's nephew, but my father's older brother was killed when your people ran my family out of Lod in 1948. Do the Jews weep for him? My family – all the Palestinian families – are the real victims. And we will have our land back. All of it. From the river to the sea."

"My mother tells me that when she was a girl, 'Palestinian' meant 'Jew' – a Jew who lived in the Holy Land. She was a Palestinian."

Dahlia looked down, returning her papers to the folder.

"This bloodshed has to stop," she said. "Don't you believe in the peace process?"

"I believe in victory."

"But seven years ago, your leaders and mine signed a peace agreement in principle. Soon they'll meet again to work out the details. Won't you welcome peace?"

"You've been honest with me, and I won't deceive you. The struggle will continue. Liberation is the goal. We don't have tanks. We don't have an air force. We will fight any way we can."

"You've been in here too long. Things have changed. There's hope for your people and mine." She paused, gathering her thoughts. "My government wants to show it believes in peace. I've been asked to recommend the release of a security prisoner as a sign of good faith."

Asfour looked thunderstruck.

"Why are you telling me this?"

"I'd like that prisoner to be you."

"Under what conditions?"

"Just that you don't do violence against us."

Asfour reflected a moment in silence.

"I can make you one promise, and I want you to listen carefully. I will never – *never!* -- return to an Israeli prison."

Dahlia smiled. "That's all we can ask, then."

4

# CHAPTER TWO

Chester County, Pennsylvania – April, 2000

"Pull over."

Frank DiRaimo spoke from the rear seat. The driver and her mother, chattering in the front, had missed it all. Now the two women glanced back at him confused.

"What?"

"Pull over," Frank said again flatly. "There's been a wreck."

Frank might have missed it too if he hadn't been so bored. The trip to Pennsylvania had been pleasant enough. Although he and Janet hadn't lived together for four years, they remained friends and he'd agreed to accompany her on a visit to her mother, who was moving from the spacious family home to a widow's apartment.

Janet had stayed behind in the condo to deal personally with the decorator, and she'd suggested that Frank have lunch with her mother and Ellen, her married sister. Ellen drove back from the restaurant through a gentle Spring rain in animated conversation with Mrs. Daniels about people Frank didn't know and mundane matters of no consequence to him. The drizzle, the mist, and the muted greens and grays were narcotic to his dreamy disposition. The windshield wipers, twin metronomes, beat a slow and hypnotic rhythm. He peered past them through the glass.

In the lane ahead, a giant semi veered left over the double line, then right in an apparent overcorrection and lumbered into a ditch. Frank watched the big rig jackknife and roll partway over. He saw no collision, and the truck hadn't been speeding. The driver must have fallen asleep.

Ellen pulled onto the shoulder. Frank jumped out, ran along the berm, and leaped over the flooded ditch. He hopped onto the right front tire and scrambled from the fender to the hood, being careful not to slip on the wet, slanted surface. A jagged hole of surprising dimensions gaped in the windshield. Frank looked into the cab. The driver, a man of about 40, was on his feet but appeared dazed.

"Can you take my arm?" Frank asked, fearing fire.

Frank edged closer, thrust his elbow through the broken glass, and braced himself as the driver grasped his forearm. Frank took up some of the man's weight and guided him through. They teetered for a moment on the hood before regaining equilibrium. Then there were voices and steadying hands on Frank's shoulders.

"The troopers are coming," one voice said.

"An ambulance is on its way," said another.

"Why didn't you tell me?" Janet demanded, incredulous. She had heard the story hours later from her relatives. "Nothing to tell, really. He was banged up but didn't seem badly hurt. Other people were there. We left."

"I feel so excluded by you, as if I mean nothing to you at all."

"What did I do to deserve that?" Frank was angered by the accusation. Hadn't he proved his friendship in a hundred ways – including coming on this trip? Now he was being criticized for aiding an accident victim, or so it seemed to him. Did he owe her a report? An explanation? A justification?

"Normal people share their experiences," she said. "They talk. It's called connection. Even when we lived together, you seemed disconnected. It felt so cold --"

"Thanks for reminding me why I moved out. I guess you found me a constant disappointment. You think I didn't feel that? You think I didn't know that you saw me as defective? I thought we could get along if we were together here for a few days. I should have known better. Talk? Share? Connect? Do you want me to talk about Vietnam? Or all the assholes at The Washington Post? You'd shut me up fast enough."

"Stop, will you? Please stop."

"Stop? You started it. I was sitting here minding my own business."

"That's the problem. Why couldn't you have told me about the truck?"

"A few minutes of clarity in a lifetime of fog? What's to tell?"

# CHAPTER THREE

Washington, D.C. – May, 2000

"For me the horror wasn't that the story was fabricated – anyone can get burned -- but that The Post and the Pulitzer committee believed it to be true and thought it was perfectly OK to protect the anonymity of people who were shooting heroin into the veins of a little boy. That's accessory to child abuse."

Frank and his editor sat at an iron mesh patio table outside a Korean buffet near Farragut Square.

"Oh, come off it!" said Tobias Moore. "You'd pass up a juicy story like that?" Moore was from London, had learned his trade at the uninhibited Fleet Street newspapers, and he brought those freewheeling ways to the Consolidated Press wire service in the United States.

"They could have had the story. It's like Mike Royko said. Nail the mother and the boyfriend. Follow the police through the door, and you've got your story. Besides, a story isn't everything."

"It isn't? Maybe you shouldn't be telling me this."

Clouds eclipsed the sun, and a gust of wind skidded an empty takeout container across the tabletop. Frank caught it before it blew off but got food residue on his fingers. He poured water from a Styrofoam cup onto a paper napkin and wiped his hands.

"Suppose a bank robber tells you: 'This is how I plan my jobs, and this is how I spend my loot. You can write about it, but you can't identify me.' Does a reporter owe confidentiality? Does he let banks get robbed to protect his source?"

"Well -- "

"OK, here's a closer parallel. Suppose a reporter learns from adults that they're prostituting a child. Wouldn't any responsible editor demand to know the names? How could you keep the identities a secret for the sake of a story? You don't owe anonymity to such people. If I were a judge, I'd lock up any journalists who invoked First Amendment privilege in a case like that. If that's the kind of reporter you expect me to be, you might as well fire me now."

"Listen," Moore said. "I expect you to develop your sources at the State Department. And when they leak to you, I'm sure it'll be in violation of some statute. And if you're too scrupulous to publish and you let yourself get scooped, I *will* fire you."

# CHAPTER FOUR

Washington, DC – May, 2000

" . . . The Oslo peace process originated within the Israeli security establishment, including elements in the army . . ."

What?

Frank's eyes widened, and he sat up in his chair. Dr. Avidan's flat affect and droning monotone had caused his attention to wander, and then Avidan dropped this clanger out of nowhere. But Avidan gave no special emphasis to his astonishing revelation, referring to it as if it were the most natural thing in the world. Or was that part of the game? Did an undercurrent of smugness flow beneath the professor's soporific delivery? Was the Israeli defense intellectual assuming the role of a bored but indulgent teacher lecturing a class of not very bright students? Frank couldn't be sure.

In the daybook that morning, Frank had seen that Avidan would speak about the Middle East peace process at a Washington think tank. He quickly decided to attend because he found himself in an unusual and awkward position: he was obligated to write about something he didn't fully understand. No matter how he tallied Oslo, he couldn't get it to add up. And if it didn't make sense to him, how could he expect his readers to fathom it?

"Soon after his reelection in 1992," Avidan continued, "Prime Minister Rabin realized that the status quo was unsustainable."

Way to psyche yourself out, Yitzhak!

Frank grew more agitated as his thoughts tumbled forth: Defeatists always say the status quo is unsustainable. For them it's perpetually five minutes to midnight. Chicken Little; the sky is falling. Oh, Mr. Prime Minister, Frank thought, remembering the assassinated leader, *mon général,* you were a fawn flushed from the undergrowth. Didn't you know it's sometimes better to sit tight than to break cover? Self-induced desperation is the most dangerous kind. Predators smell panic, no matter how elegantly the prey rationalizes its fear. Folly!

"The PLO had emerged from the Madrid Conference as the legitimate representative of the Palestinian people," Avidan went on, "and the world seemed to judge Israel according to its willingness to make peace."

Who cares what the world thinks?

Exasperation churned Frank's gut. Did the world care when the Nazis slaughtered Jews by the millions and the British slammed shut the doors of Palestine? Even Winston Churchill, who liked Jews and was sympathetic to Zionism, did nothing to change this policy as wartime prime minister. The whole point of having a Jewish state, Frank reminded himself, is not worrying about what the nations think. If Israel ever accepts the idea that its legitimacy depends on world opinion, the game is up.

Sometimes people asked Frank if his mother was Jewish. In fact he wasn't Jewish at all, but Israel had captured his imagination in his early teens. And although he had Jewish friends and acquaintances in high school, only he among them was interested in Israel. They were hardheaded realists -- future physicists, federal judges and gastroenterologists -- but Frank was a romantic, a storyteller. The Zionist dream appealed to his visionary and idealistic nature.

Who could recall a greater historical adventure? A 3,000-year-old people, the victim of the greatest act of mass murder ever committed on the planet, has the indomitable will to reconstitute itself in its ancient homeland, to revive its ancient language, to assert its right to live, to create new life, to nourish and maintain it in defiance of all odds. There's never been anything like it before, Frank thought, and there never will be again.

"Israel's leadership realized that the country is surrounded by two concentric circles," Avidan explained patiently. "The inner circle is made up of its immediate neighbors: Egypt, Jordan, Syria, Lebanon, and by extension Saudi Arabia."

Frank listened attentively.

"The outer circle includes Iran, Iraq and Afghanistan to the east, Sudan, Somalia and Yemen to the south, and Libya to the west. Almost all are rogue states, and some revealed early nuclear ambitions.

"The best minds in Israel realized that Iranian-sponsored Islamic fundamentalism constitutes a threat to the inner circle no less than to Israel itself. By 1992 Islamic fundamentalism -- which still is trying to destabilize the Gulf Emirates -- already had created havoc in Syria, Algeria, Egypt, Jordan, in the Horn of Africa and in Yemen. And it was gaining influence in the West Bank and in the Gaza Strip, where Iran was pouring millions in the form of social welfare and health and education programs.

"Further, the fundamentalists were doing everything they could to turn a political struggle between Jews and Arabs into a religious conflict – Muslim against Jew, Islam against Judaism. And while political struggles can be solved by negotiation and compromise, theological conflict has no solution. Then it's jihad, religious war, their God against our God.

"Therefore," and here Avidan allowed a trace of satisfaction to creep into his voice, "it became apparent that a confluence of interest had arisen between Israel and the inner circle of countries. But how was Israel to capitalize on this momentous opportunity for partnership with its immediate neighbors? Only one way. Make peace with the Palestinians! Yasser Arafat and his PLO were the last vestige of secular Palestinian nationalism. Israel had no one else to deal with. It was the PLO or nothing."

Frank squirmed and stifled a groan. Too clever by half, he thought. Jews outsmarting themselves. Jews with too much time on their hands. Inner circles and outer circles, cockamamie abstractions. An imaginary confluence of interest with people who hate you. Wishful thinking. Unbelievable. Only Jews could talk themselves from a position of strength to one of supplicating their worst enemies. Imagine! To make a gang of murderers, car thieves, and extortionists indispensible to your existence. "Excuse us, but we can't seem to live without you. Would you please be so kind as to accept our terms of surrender?" From what Frank knew about Arabs, this wasn't a good strategy. And Israelis, more than anyone, should understand Arabs. But what was that phrase? Did Jabotinsky say it? "You can take the Jew out of the exile, but you can't take the exile out of the Jew." Arafat was a bandit chief -- an Egyptian assassin -- not some Polish gentleman who could be appeased, humored, and cajoled.

Avidan concluded his remarks and opened the floor for questions. Frank resisted his impulse to bolt, feeling obliged to stay till the end. He never had been to the Middle East, and he hoped some old Levantine hand would challenge Avidan's assumptions. Nothing doing. Frank had been present when some of the journalists in the room had interrogated people in what he considered to be an unnecessarily rude and argumentative manner. Now they were pussycats. Their questions were trite, superficial, uncritical, and deferential. Perhaps soon Frank would confront the delusions that dripped with haughty assurance from Avidan's lips, but not today. He needed time to process what he had learned and to gather more information.

Frank packed his tape recorder and notebook into his briefcase. The six-block walk to the State Department would give him time to think. Should he write a story based on Avidan's talk or use it only as background? He'd decide presently.

Frank donned his raincoat and walked out to the street. The drizzle felt good on his face, and the cooler outside air – although clammy and tainted with vehicle exhaust – was welcome.

He never would have guessed that Oslo was a self-inflicted wound. Rather, he would have blamed the detestable foreign policy "realists" for putting the muscle on Rabin: the execrable James A. Baker III, the dubious Brent Scowcroft – or, from the Democratic side, the toxic residue of Zbigniew Brzezinski, a relic from the Carter administration.

In 1993, when Yitzhak Rabin shook Yasser Arafat's hand on the White House lawn and signed the Oslo Accords, Frank had been a copy editor in The Washington Post's Editorial Department. The ostentatious display of false fraternity had made him queasy. If his more sanguine colleagues had taken any notice, they would have attributed Frank's mood to his mordant manner and saturnine personality. Being critical made him a good editor. Anything that existed could be improved, and he could spot the flaw that others missed. But this didn't make him an easy man to live with.

In any case, the Oslo agreement wasn't Frank's to accept or reject, and nobody cared what he thought. Even so, he felt the need to have a position on matters important to him. But what good was it to fuss? Rabin had put the full weight of his military prestige behind the peace agreement. Rabin was a former army chief of staff – the top soldier during Israel's stunning victory in the 1967 Six-Day War. He was a member of the Jewish State's founding generation. Surely, Rabin knew what he was doing. Didn't he?

Frank was vaguely aware that things hadn't gone right in the years following the Oslo signings, but detailed knowledge of the Middle East had not been one of his responsibilities at The Post. He'd have to refresh his memory.

A horn blared, and Frank lurched back to the curb. He had the right of way, but an impatient driver making a right turn on a red light didn't want to wait for a moping pedestrian. Frank felt a flash of anger. He wanted to yell back, but the driver had his window closed and was out of earshot anyway.

# CHAPTER FIVE

Lunchtime brought faint growls of hunger. Frank approached the turnstile at the State Department's 23rd Street entrance, swiped his pass card, and walked against the bar. The steel cylinder, immobile, assailed his thighs. He looked up at the guard, who shrugged. He tried the card again, and this time the turnstile gave way with a satisfying clunk.

Frank turned to his right, passed through another secure doorway and walked down the hall to the press center, where he would leave his coat and briefcase before going to the cafeteria. He still had time to eat before the daily news briefing.

The capacious Consolidated Press and Associated Press offices, roughly equal in size, were at opposite ends of the cavernous newsroom. Reporters from other news agencies toiled in the open area between. This allocation of space was all that remained of a reality that had existed 40 years before, when

CP had been a major news source. Without a doubt, the AP still merited its privileged status. It was the largest and most respected wire service, and newspapers big and small relied on its top-flight copy. Two dignified, experienced, and well-tailored diplomatic correspondents labored diligently in the AP's shipshape office, producing reports read around the world.

"This place is a fucking mess," Frank thought again as he entered the Consolidated Press's office. Desolation. The casual observer would justly wonder if the space had been abandoned years before. Despite Frank's few possessions and a pile of his papers, the office looked derelict, forsaken, and cluttered with the detritus of decades. The bookshelves held the abandoned volumes of a score of his predecessors. The broadcast booth, testimony to happier times, was waist high with junk visible through the window. On Frank's first day as CP's State Department correspondent, he had peered through the glass and spotted a forlorn headset on a shelf where the transmitter must have sat. He never opened the door. Stacks of papers, unbound monographs, and obsolete reports occupied every surface. Half-empty file cabinets held long forgotten time sheets and expense claims. The furniture, including his desk chair, was falling apart.

Still, Frank had eked out a small workspace amid the chaos. He didn't think it was his place to rehabilitate the office, a mammoth undertaking that would have consumed innumerable days off. How could he bring a dumpster onto State Department grounds? And how could he determine what to throw away, what to save, and what to shred?

What he really needed was a printer. His research style was more ethnographic than journalistic. He typed and printed out full transcriptions of his interviews. He sifted through Internet reports, highlighting sentences, comparing perspectives, and reaching his conclusions after shuffling through sheaves of paper. His efforts to wheedle a printer out of the main office had been unsuccessful, and he was considering buying one himself for the bureau.

Frank heard rumors of State Department plans to renovate the press center, stripping CP of its envied office space and assigning it a cubicle commensurate with its reduced significance. No one was sure when this would happen. In the meantime, Frank appreciated the privacy. He hated having people overhear his phone calls and didn't want to listen to the chatter of others.

Frank had been assigned to the State Department only for a short time and didn't know how long his franchise would run. Even in CP's glory years, even when it had hundreds of subscribers, even before the demise of the evening papers it was designed to serve, the wire service had lost money every year but one. "Wire service!" The words themselves were archaic. Who sent telegrams anymore?

The deceased owner, scion of a Midwestern newspaper baron, had run Consolidated Press as a vanity news source, essentially as a philanthropy. After the heir's death, lawyers told his survivors that if they continued to subsidize the CP in the manner of their late father, the conglomerate's stockholders could sue them for dereliction of their fiduciary duty to the company. So, almost 20 years ago, the survivors had stripped CP of its assets and sold it off.

Thus began a series of unfortunate sales to progressively less competent owners. And with each change of hands, the wire service got smaller and smaller. "No news organization ever cut its way to profitability," observed Tobias Moore, Frank's editor at CP's headquarters near the White House. Now only an English-language Asian broadsheet carried CP's copy. Frank wasn't sure where else it went. People Frank interviewed often asked, understandably, where the story would appear. He gave them the address of a vagabond Web site where Frank would go to look for his own stuff. But even this free access pulled in few readers. The current editor in chief was trying to find a buyer who would take a renewed, restored, and profitable Consolidated Press into the electronic age. Frank wished him luck.

# CHAPTER SIX

As Frank passed through the press center on his way to the corridor, a small gray specter tugged at his sleeve and emitted muffled sounds. It was Mitzi Horowitz with her mouth full. With imploring eyes and the furtive movements of a forest creature, the older woman led him to a cubicle where scavenged sandwich triangles, cookies, and pastry bits rested on paper napkins. Clearly, Mitzi had been to a briefing where food was served. Many reporters were poorly paid, and most were not above scrounging a lunch, but Mitzi was in a class by herself. Now, like a lioness with her kill, Mitzi was sharing her repast.

Frank knew Mitzi intended him to see this as a mark of special favor. Of all the journalists covering the State Department, the snacks were for him alone. In the short time he had been on the beat, she had attempted to make an ally of him. No one knew who Mitzi worked for, where her stories appeared, or how she got press credentials to both the State Department and the White House. But despite her uncertain status, she was able to score interviews with the highest officials, and occasionally she made Frank aware of events he otherwise would have overlooked. They would share a cab, cadge lunch, and Frank would put the taxi fare on his expense account. Sometimes there even was a story in it. Perhaps he was selling her short as a journalist.

But Mitzi was conspiratorial. She acted as if it were she and Frank against the world. She told him whom he could trust and whom to be wary of, and some of her advice surprised him. She showed him an eight-by-ten-inch glossy black-and-white photo of herself with Eleanor Roosevelt in 1961.

"See how cute I was?"

And she had been very cute indeed. But now she was a tiny, wizened old woman with bad teeth that gave her trouble when she ate, sometimes with embarrassing spatters. Once when Frank worked late, Mitzi asked him to walk her to her apartment house – which he did, saying goodbye at the door. Frank didn't assume Mitzi was engaging in a ruse, but rather that she wanted the protection afforded by the company of a large man. On the other hand, she had become indignant when Rachael Fletcher, a glamorous ABC News reporter, playfully flirted with Frank, flashing her cleavage in his face.

Frank was ambivalent about all this. He suspected that he was only the latest in a series of "best friends" Mitzi had tried to cultivate. Mitzi was a marginal figure among the reporters – something of a joke, although no one was cruel to her – and he was marginal enough himself as a 56-year-old cub reporter for a moribund news agency. He shuddered to think that Mitzi might be drawn to him by her perception of their mutual marginality -- two misfits, outcasts together, loyal to the end. His feelings toward her were genuinely friendly, but he considered her a little paranoid and a bit of a nut. He didn't want to be drawn farther into her orbit, and he didn't want to be identified with her too closely.

He thanked her for offering him the food. Not wanting to spoil his appetite for the hot meal he anticipated, he smiled and nibbled at a salmon-and-dill canapé.

"I'll come back later for a cookie," he said. "But don't save it. Only if there's one left."

Nearby voices caught Frank's attention, and the words "Arafat" and "Sharm El-Sheikh" put him on alert. A handful of reporters had gathered around the desk of Brett Lynn, State Department correspondent for Agence France-Presse, the French news agency. Brett always was worth listening to. Young and charismatic, he was an engaging raconteur. Frank had observed that people from the Great Lakes region possessed an acute awareness of the absurd. Brett was from Buffalo and Frank was from Cleveland, so Frank could relate to the younger man's arch sense of humor.

Although Brett looked every inch the Celto-Saxon – tall, with sandy hair, light eyes and a ruddy complexion -- the surname Lynn was an inheritance from Lin, a long-ago Chinese ancestor. Frank sensed that Eleanor MacDougal -- the dangerously attractive Scottish brunette who was one of Reuter's two diplomatic correspondents -- had a crush on Brett, who seemed oblivious of it. If a woman like Eleanor had shown any real interest in *me*, Frank thought, they would have had to throw a net over me to keep me off her. And now, there she stood among Brett's appreciative listeners.

With a tilt of the head, Frank signaled to Mitzi that they should edge over to the conclave.

"Have you ever been to the seafood restaurant next to Arafat's headquarters in Gaza?" Frank heard Brett ask someone. "It's pretty good, considering."

Frank surmised that Brett was referring to the agreement signed eight months before at Sharm El-Sheikh, in the Egyptian Sinai. Brett must have been one of the reporters who accompanied Secretary of State Madeleine Albright on that trip the previous September, when Frank still was at The Washington Post.

"Basically, the agreement was negotiated in Gaza," Brett said. "That's what Albright was trying to get them to do. We got there in the evening, had dinner at this restaurant next door and waited in the hold room. The meeting went on and on and on. It got to be 10 o'clock, then 11 o'clock. And there was this Arafat aide who kept coming down and announcing to all the journalists sitting there: 'Two minutes! Maybe three.' Over and over. Finally, somebody asked: 'An American two minutes, or a Palestinian two minutes?'

"Anyway, at last they came down and announced they had reached an agreement and everyone would be going to Sharm the next day to sign it under Mubarak's auspices. We were to drive back to Jerusalem and catch a plane the next morning.

"So we finally get out of there. It's well after midnight. Gaza at the best of times doesn't have great electricity or roads.

"But none of us knows what the hell is in the agreement, so Albright's people say: 'Okay, we'll have Dennis ride in the press van with you on the way back to Jerusalem, because there really isn't any other time for him to brief you. When we get back we're going to have maybe two hours' sleep, and then we're getting on the plane for Sharm.' "

Dennis? Frank guessed this was a reference to Dennis Ross. Frank was vaguely aware that Ross was President Clinton's Middle East envoy, but as yet he'd formed no clear impression of the man.

"So there's this mad rush for the motorcade, everyone piles in, and Dennis finally gets in. Unfortunately, in the confusion, the motorcade took off without us."

Brett paused to let the alarmed voices subside.

"So Albright's press people are, like, *frantic*. We've got to get back into the motorcade because we have to cross back into Israel. And if we're not in the motorcade, we ain't going to cross back in. Right? So Albright's people are screaming at this poor Palestinian driver who understands maybe three words of English. He's careening through the narrow streets of Gaza trying to catch up with the motorcade. We get lost at one point. There are very few streetlights, and he's blasting the horn. Donkeys are skittering off, bicyclists are diving out of the way, and we're bouncing off the inside of the mini-bus.

"And in the back, we're all trying to listen to Dennis explain this deal. And we're literally being thrown around. It was basically complete chaos. With the honking of the horn and the press aides yelling at the poor driver, it was almost impossible to hear.

"Anyway, amid all the confusion, Dennis holds forth with this very long-winded and useless explanation about how both sides will have to give. And we're thinking: 'Yeah, yeah. Who gives what, exactly?' In that monotone of his, he says nobody's going to get 100 percent. The typical Dennis kind of bullshit.

And then he starts with the old crap about our foreign policy being like three legs of a stool. And Morrie just lost his shit. He said, 'Goddamn it, Dennis. Just tell us what's in the fucking agreement!' "

A wave of appreciative laughter broke over the room. Apparently, many of those present also had been on the receiving end of Ross's foggy obfuscations. And everyone knew that the AP's Morris Gordon was a consummate pro.

"Dennis looked very chagrined and then did a little better job, but not great," Brett concluded. "We got back to Jerusalem without a huge amount of knowledge about what was in this deal."

# CHAPTER SEVEN

F rank decided on the spaghetti line. Customers holding bowls of vegetables and cold cuts queued up like refugees along the stainless steel rail. As their turn came, they would choose their sauce and pasta shape and hand the bowl to a small, fierce woman who combined the three elements on a steaming grill, where several fragrant heaps cooked simultaneously.

Frank regarded the furiously industrious woman with guilt and respect. She probably wasn't much older than he but showed a lot more mileage. As she kept the line moving, Frank read both fatigue and indomitability on her face. Washington had no white, working-class neighborhoods, so he pictured her getting up at an ungodly hour to commute from a distant suburb. He wondered how late she had to stay after her shift to clean up her section.

Next to her, I'm just a spoiled college boy, Frank told himself. Although his grandparents had been penniless immigrants, economic refugees to the United States, his father had done well, sparing his children this woman's drudgery. As a student Frank had worked because he thought he should, not out of necessity. In high school he was a stock boy in a department store. In college he clerked in a drugstore and delivered prescriptions in the pharmacist's Dodge. Carrying sandbags and ammunition boxes in Vietnam didn't count, nor did those few times he had humped the field radio on patrol. Except for one sweltering day clambering over bins of inventory in the upper floors of a Cleveland warehouse, he never had to work as hard as the woman preparing his lunch.

Frank fumbled with his change at the cashier's station and began his search for a place to sit. The vast lunchroom with its obtrusive pillars seemed unusually crowded. He would have preferred a small table where he could sit with his back to a wall and have a clear view of the entrances.

"Do you think you have PTSD?" a friend from Cleveland, a fellow veteran, had asked him.

"If I do, I got it in the United States," Frank said.

A soldier with Post Traumatic Stress Disorder? Or a debutante with Post Dramatic Dress Disorder? Not a dime's worth of difference to the bicoastal and academic elites.

# PART TWO

# CHAPTER EIGHT

Frank was not naïve about war when he arrived in Vietnam in the spring of 1967. Of course, no one's ever fully prepared. Killing one's fellow humans is beastly business, whether you're inflicting the violence or receiving it. Even so, Vietnam held no real surprises for Frank.

But what awaited him upon his return had left him shocked, numbed, dumbfounded, enraged, disoriented, and temporarily ineffective. Because what Frank experienced had no historical precedent, he was utterly unready for it. It hadn't happened to returning Confederate soldiers or to German veterans of either world war. America's intellectual and artistic elite – the most stylish and influential elements of his own society -- along with a sizable minority of Frank's fellow citizens, actively disdained Vietnam veterans and lost no opportunity to express their contempt.

He still seethed with cold fury from that betrayal. He held no grudge against the Viet Cong or the North Vietnamese. Why should he? But his own people -- that was something else. The fear of physical annihilation in Vietnam was nothing compared to the pain of social nullification in the United States.

If Frank had gone from Vietnam to a steel mill in Birmingham, Alabama, the transition would have been less brutal. Instead he studied history in the graduate school of a large northeastern university. The professors, even the militant leftists, mostly were polite and fair. Some were World War II veterans whose approval Frank would have welcomed. It hurt him to know that, to them, the real heroes of the Vietnam War were the unhygienic draft dodgers and mangy student protestors.

The grad students were another story. Frank made some friends among them, but he never felt fully accepted and he never fully accepted them. Having taken the trouble to avoid Vietnam, the men were compelled, unconsciously, to denigrate his service. They were not fully aware of their dismissive asides, passive aggression, and subtle insults. Others, however, were flat-out sons of bitches. They rationalized their shirking by asserting that Vietnam was an illegal and immoral war, and anyone "complicit" in it was either immoral or stupid. No subtlety or passivity tempered their hostility.

Frank could have achieved a measure of redemption among the women by presenting himself as a victim.

"Were you drafted?" they would ask charitably.

Frank would explain that he had enlisted in an environment of conscription, but it would have been easy to get out. An angle was available to almost everybody. You just had to work it.

"For example, I had borderline high blood pressure. I could have come in clutching a doctor's note honestly attesting to that. I could have taken amphetamines before the physical exam, and my blood pressure would have been through the roof. As it was they almost didn't take me."

"Then why did you go?"

"I knew that with my smart mouth and snarky attitude, I'd last about 45 minutes in a communist country before they dragged me off. Why should the Vietnamese have less freedom? We had a treaty with those people. They were allies! Vietnam was no different from Korea except the aggression was incremental. And why should others go and I skate out?"

Frank didn't change anyone's mind, nor did he expect to. Nevertheless, he was determined to live up to his beliefs and to bear witness to the truth as he understood it. He was willing to pay the price, even if the cost was high.

He dated in graduate school, but only a couple of relationships amounted to anything. There was the false start with the artist, a divorced mother of a six-year-old girl. Even though they might have been mismatched, he knew in retrospect that he could have handled things better.

More serious was his engagement to a polyglot New England WASP who was getting her PhD in anthropology. There, he reflected, the match had been unusually good. So why did the engagement fizzle? Why did she pull away in the end? His moods, irritability and impatience certainly had played a part. And, 27 years later, he was beginning to understand that his neediness, both emotional and sexual, probably left her feeling drained, used, and resentful. Of course, she had her issues too. Frank was wild about her, but his friends had found her cold and aloof.

He married Sandy on the bounce. The anguish of losing the woman he thought was his life partner manifested itself physically. Sometimes it was dry heaves. His tension headaches returned. He first had them as a boy when he understood, inchoately, that his parents considered him an imposition. The headaches came back in Vietnam when he realized, finally, that his government wasn't serious about winning the war. The North Vietnamese, he knew, *were* serious. Ergo, the war was lost. But just as he had been stuck with his parents, so was he stuck in Vietnam.

The headaches would begin in the late morning and build throughout the day, accompanied by growing nausea, sensitivity to light, and an abhorrence of cooking smells. The muscles at the base of his skull would knot and throb, and in the evening he would vomit. Strangely, after that he would feel better.

He decided to refresh his mind and spirit with a fishing trip to Minnesota. He had been there years before and had loved the sparkling lakes and deep green forests. His return to the woods didn't disappoint him. Communing with nature refreshed his soul and lifted his depression. Fresh air and the call of the loons exhilarated him.

He spotted Sandy at the bait shop. He had been examining some local maps when he became aware of a conversation at the cash register. He looked up to see Sandy give a broad smile to two middle-aged men he took to be tourists. He was hungry for such a smile. When was the last time one had come his way?

He eased his way over to the counter, pretending to be interested in fishhooks, lures, socks, raingear, rubber boots, and lacquered pine medallions inscribed with folksy sayings. He doubled back to the maps and selected one. His eyes fell on a cooler, from which he extracted a tuna sandwich and a small carton of orange juice. Fortified with these pretexts, he strode to the cash register with renewed confidence.

Her smile was less certain than the one she had lavished on the tourists, but she answered his questions amiably enough.

"Do you think we'll get a storm?"

"Maybe tomorrow."

"Any moose in this area?"

"Yes, some."

"I'm thinking about coming back in the fall with an out-of-state permit."

"You'll have fun. Dress warm."

"Is it too far south for woodland caribou?"

She handed him his change with a puzzled look.

"I think they used to be here, but nobody's seen one in a long time. You can't hunt them. There's no season."

Frank castigated himself for a bungler. She's a cashier, he reminded himself, not a forest ranger. Don't be creepy!

"Are you from around here? Beautiful country."

She really wasn't bad looking: medium height, long dark hair in bangs, startling blue eyes, wide full-lipped mouth, fair complexion, and a figure both slim and curvy. He didn't usually like bangs, but on her they looked cute.

"Yes, just down the road."

He scanned her left hand for a wedding band. Few university women her age would have been married, but he knew rural and small-town people paired off younger. No ring.

Frank sensed that the small talk had reached a critical juncture. He could break it off or go for broke.

"Say, I'm going to be here for a few more days. Would you like to join me in getting something to eat?"

Silence. Frank could hear the shuffle of other customers lining up behind him.

"Sure, that would be nice."

Her answer came as a surprise. He'd been ready for the sorry-but-I-have-a-boyfriend brush-off.

One thing led to another, including a lakeside tryst on a beach towel followed the next night by another in his cabin. Then it was time to go. The semester was about to begin, and he had duties as a teaching assistant.

Ten years earlier, the interval between hello and vaginal intercourse might have been longer, but it already was the 1970s, and the Age of Aquarius had dawned. (As discreetly as possible, Frank asked Sandy if she had the contraceptive base covered. Sure enough, she was on the pill.)

As a student of history, Frank knew that social change was in the natural order of things. But he also knew of no advanced society that had changed as rapidly as his own just in the past few years. The world that existed when Frank left for the Army in mid-1966 was almost unrecognizable when he returned late in 1969. Of all the transmutations, the only one that didn't grate on him was that women now were more available for sex. But even this gave him vague misgivings. All he ever had wanted was to be in a loving marriage – with lots of great sex, to be sure. Was this new ethos conducive to that? He put the thought out of his mind. He had remained a virgin till he was 24 in the hope that he would sleep with only one woman in his life. He had been chaste even when on R&R in Bangkok, spending his time in jewelry stores designing an engagement ring for the wife he one day hoped to have. He believed he had made an honest effort to uphold traditional family structure. He felt that in his own small way he had discharged his duty to the collective. He still hoped to settle down with someone really special, but the rules had changed. Would he ever find her? How long could he wait in tortured, touch-starved celibacy? In the meantime, he would take his pleasures where he found them, and he hoped that he gave as much pleasure as he got. Even Steven. That was fair -- wasn't it?

# CHAPTER NINE

F rank wasn't surprised when Sandy asked if they would write. Even so, he was forced to hide his ambivalence when he assented to give her his address. A part of him wanted to make a clean getaway. On the other hand, he was reluctant to give her cause to see herself as a woman wronged – seduced and abandoned. Callousness was not part of his nature. He wanted her to see that. And he didn't need more guilt. From the distance of half a continent, what harm could a few letters do? She'd probably lose interest soon enough. Another guy was sure to come along shortly.

But guilt overtook him when he found himself wishing he had vanished from Minnesota like a thief in the night. Sandy's letters made him feel like he had stolen something. Not her virginity, surely, but some unascertained commodity. Her attempt to maintain contact with him was transparently sincere but pedestrian and infelicitous. Her chatty letters bored him, and he found annoying her habit of referring to people he didn't know as if he'd been potty trained with them. How hard was it to identify Susan as her high school friend or John as her sister's husband?

He kept his replies brief and businesslike. "Who's Ruth?" he wrote. "Who's Marty? I have no way of knowing who these people are."

"Your tone is so cold," she wrote back. Then the dread words: "Frank, what about us?"

Us?

"Whats going to happen with this thing we have going?"

Thing?

What's going to happen with the missing apostrophe?

Years later he came to wish he had replied that "there is no us" and "we have no thing," but at the time he didn't have the heart to do it. It seemed so cruel. Perhaps more important, he wasn't doing that well with women in his own circles. What had seemed a promising beginning with a PhD candidate in political science flamed out after a couple of months, leaving him confused and dejected. He was getting tired of neurotic, indignant, resentful university women. Sandy was so sweet, so uncomplicated, so wholesome.

Maybe he wasn't giving her a fair chance. It's true that she smoked. And if she read at all, it was romance novels. But who was Frank to be so high and mighty? He was no better than she. He wrote back suggesting a visit to Minnesota during the Thanksgiving holiday.

It went better than he had expected. Sandy's parents and siblings were salt of the earth. The local people embodied heartland values. The Vietnam War, dragging on interminably, was not popular, but to the extent that his military service counted at all, it was a slight plus. And, in the short time he was there, he and Sandy deepened their connection.

Frank returned to the university with a growing distaste for his existence as a graduate student. He felt like Kevin McCarthy at the end of "Invasion of the Body Snatchers." It was as if space aliens had stolen the essence of those around him, leaving behind only corporeal husks programmed to act out bizarre roles.

He was sick to death of angry feminists, identity politicians, structural Marxists, neo-pagan nature-worshippers, French post-structuralists, queer theorists, affirmative action hustlers, co-eds in tiny apartments with pregnant dogs, black militants, Che Guevara posters, urban guerrillas, Mao caps, liberation theology, Trotskyite revanchists, Hegelian dialecticians, postmodern parlor pinks, smug street theater, recreational drug use, psychedelic anything, and the campus chapter of Vietnam Veterans Against the War.

Frank's fellow academicians acclaimed Herbert Marcuse for asserting that although capitalist democracies were tolerant, they were guilty of "repressive tolerance." Clearly, this was moronic – a hallucination if Marcuse believed it and a crude hoax if he didn't. But the people surrounding Frank hailed Marcuse as an oracle. And they swooned for Noam Chomsky's "transformational generative grammar," which was no better than a carnival scam. (What was new was not valuable, and what was valuable was not new.) Groovy professors were making fools of themselves in pathetic efforts to be more avant-garde than their students. Bored Bohemian ironists in black turtlenecks showcased their ennui by blowing smoke rings with French cigarettes. It was time for a change.

Frank knew that arranged marriages had been the norm until relatively recently, and he had read interviews of the widows of such arrangements. "But did you love him?" was the inevitable question. "I *learned* to love him," was the invariable response. Frank had nobody to fix him up, so he would arrange his own marriage. To Sandy. He would learn to love her! He decided to leave the doctoral program after getting a master's degree. He moved to Minnesota, married Sandy, and taught at a junior college. In six years together, they had a boy and a girl. Her bipolarity, hypochondria, and heavy drinking were not apparent to him until after the wedding.

He hated every cigarette she smoked, and it showed on his face. He hated himself for being bored, irritated and impatient with her, for lacking the backbone to hide it, and for yielding to the compulsion to show others, in front of her, that she was beneath him. With eye-rolls and asides, he signaled that her banal preoccupations and kitschy taste were not his and shouldn't be construed as a reflection on him. And he was mortified by the inevitable and justified disgust this evoked in others.

"Do you know how unattractive you are when you do that?" a woman colleague said to him one day. He knew then that the marriage would have to end.

He decided to return to the university for his doctorate. Frank was relieved when Sandy said that she and the children wouldn't go with him. He saw a lawyer who drew up a separation agreement. Don was four years old, and Laura was almost two.

# CHAPTER TEN

He kept up with the kids with phone calls and letters with cuttings from the Sunday comics. He mailed them cassette tapes of him reading children's stories. He even sang to them on one tape. But it was no substitute for being a father, and he knew it.

During his time with Sandy, he had continued with his historical research, so he was able to catch up on course work, write his PhD dissertation and defend it in only 18 months. He taught as an adjunct at the university while looking for a tenure-track position. It was a bad time to be job-hunting in academia. The training of graduate students brought professors prestige, so PhDs were proliferating at a geometric rate. Almost 180 candidates competed for the assistant professorship Frank eventually secured at a Midwestern college. It was 1982. He was almost 39 years old.

Life at the college was tolerable. Although admission was not particularly selective, the top 15 percent of the students there were as good as students anywhere. The pay was a pittance, but some of the older faculty members were simpatico as well as a few of the younger ones. But most of the professors his age seemed ill at ease around him. Frank didn't call attention to his Vietnam service, but neither did he hide it. He came to understand that his very presence was a rebuke to them.

One day a psychologist from a distant university came to the campus to give an address on his groundbreaking research, and Frank was assigned to show him around before the presentation. At lunch the man revealed that he had served in the 1st Marine Air Wing in Danang. Frank told him his impressions of the younger male faculty.

"They're afraid of us," the psychologist said.

"What?"

"They're afraid of us."

"Why should they be afraid?" Frank asked, sensing that the man might be on to something. "What are they afraid of?"

"They're afraid of us physically."

"But we're not going to do anything to them."

"Of course, but it's visceral. It's not a rational fear. It's a phobia. Emotional. I've seen it a lot."

This gave Frank something to think about. Eventually, these phobic men – who had been in grad school when he was in Vietnam and were accruing academic seniority when he was toiling at the junior college – would evaluate him for tenure. He was back in the belly of the beast.

He began attending services at a nondenominational church as a way of meeting women, and he got lucky. Audrey had worked for the CIA in the Saigon embassy. Observing decorum, Frank never asked about her duties there. She since had soured on the war, but so what? She pretty much kept it to herself. He considered Audrey to be a comrade in arms. Long after they met, he was not surprised to learn that she was a Mensa member. They dated for the two years he was at the college.

Frank missed his kids, and he knew that growing up fatherless exacts a toll. He called Sandy and asked if she would be willing to relocate. He couldn't afford a second household, but maybe he could find a place for her with another single mother. She agreed.

At first the arrangement worked well. It was wonderful to be in the same town as the children and to spend time with them, and it seemed to mean a lot to the kids that he was near. They adjusted nicely to their new school.

But then things fell apart. Sandy had lost her license after her second DWI and was not the type to rely on public transportation. The calls would come at the most inconvenient times. "We're out of milk," she'd say. Or, "we're low on groceries." Or, "the kids need shoes." He then would feel obligated to drop what he was doing and drive them around. Sandy took delight in walking through the malls together with him and the kids, reveling in strangers' assumptions that they were an intact family. She would drag out the shopping trips almost till closing time, when the kids should have been in bed. There always was another store to check out and more pizza slices to buy. Frank felt manipulated and as enraged as a trapped animal.

Properly motivated and with a modicum of organization, Sandy could have done her shopping during the day while he was at work. But she correctly sensed that he was involved with another woman, and she used provisioning the children as a way to pull him back. He couldn't bring himself to say: "Without milk? Low on groceries? Well, I guess you'll have to figure out what to do." Much later he wished that he had.

Sandy fell out with her roommate, accusing the woman of stealing from her. Knowing Sandy's penchant for losing things, and recalling her false accusations in the past, Frank thought this unlikely. But from then on the atmosphere in the apartment was poisoned.

After several months, when it became clear that Frank wouldn't return to her, Sandy began complaining that she missed her family and friends in Minnesota. She had custody. Frank couldn't force her to stay. He resolved never to live in the same town as Sandy. He would stay out of her reach and not put himself at her mercy again. He hoped the kids would understand some day.

On a cold winter night, with the snow crunching underfoot, Frank put Sandy and the kids and their belongings on a Greyhound bus. At first it looked like there was no room for Don's sled. The anguish on the little boy's face tore at Frank's heart. He never would forgive Sandy for this.

The call from a rest stop woke him at 2:00 a.m. "Your daughter is crying for you. What should I do?"

Had she planned this? Sandy's apartment was forfeit. If she got on the next bus back, there was only one place she and the kids could go. They would have to move in with Frank. Sandy was using Laura's tears as a means of soliciting the invitation from him. Not in a thousand years, he thought. Not if you were the last woman on Earth. For once Frank showed some sense.

"You've got to do what you think is right," he said.

After an awkward silence, she mumbled something and the line went dead. Sandy continued on her way.

# CHAPTER ELEVEN

Toward the end of the second semester, a young man appeared in Frank's office.

"Dr. DiRaimo, you're a Vietnam veteran, right?

"Yes."

Then, in one breath: "I've been offered an ROTC scholarship, and-I-want-to know-if-you-had-to-do-it-over-again-would-you-do-it-over-again-yes-or-no?"

Frank was stunned. If, five minutes earlier, someone had posited the existence of a hypothetical student with a hypothetical question, his answer would have been: "Hell no! Let them find another sucker next time."

But this was a real student with a real question that demanded a real answer. And until that moment, he hadn't known what it was.

"Yeah," Frank said. "Yes, I would."

A tear, taking Frank by surprise, streamed down his cheek, and the boy couldn't help but notice. The tear was for all that had been lost and in gratitude that some of it might be redeemed in the person of this fine young man.

The student thanked him and departed.

Frank told the dean that the next academic year would be his last at the college. Full professors who had been there 20 years were making only a little more than he. And could he even expect a fair shot at being promoted on schedule? He already was far behind his age peers, and in six more years he would face a tenure committee made up of score-settling passive-aggressives.

But, more important, he felt that he had sidelined himself. He was a big-picture guy – macro, not micro. And the big picture he wanted to understand was how his government could have fouled up the Vietnam War so badly. He had grown up believing that, in Washington, a cadre of distinguished leaders behind closed doors knew what it was doing. Clearly, this was not the case, and the result was a lost war.

Frank found the stereotypical "competitive" American male to be faintly ridiculous. How could anyone get worked up over a golf game, or a tennis match, or a loss by the home team? But one thing stirred Frank's competitive juices: He didn't like losing wars. If he was involved in one, he wanted to win. Who screwed that up? He needed to find out, and he needed to pass this knowledge down to the younger generation in a medium accessible to them.

Frank had always wanted his work to have a visual dimension. Maybe he could make a documentary film. He'd go to Washington and interview those who made the policy decisions. Why didn't you cut the Ho Chi Minh Trail? Why didn't you bring the full force of U.S. air and naval power to bear? Why didn't you isolate the battlefield? Why did you leave the initiative to the enemy?

The idea took shape during the next academic year, when he also realized that he was getting flat as a teacher. He would yawn during his own lectures. It wasn't fair to the students.

In a final act of friendship, Audrey helped him pack his car. She was an exceptional woman, she had helped him in many ways, and he always would be grateful to her. But, good as it was, the relationship didn't anchor him in place.

Maybe it was her habit of giving little digs and then, high-mindedly, playing the grownup and quickly changing the subject, leaving Frank off-balance, feeling dismissed, patronized, and infantilized. "Did she just say that?" he would wonder. "Does it mean what I think it means? Even if it's partly true, it's not the whole story."

But by then Audrey would be on to other things. Any attempt to ask for a clarification, to offer an explanation, or to provide context would be met by the sharp edge of her tongue. Frank found Audrey a little intimidating when she was snappish, and he wasn't easily intimidated. She'd use her high intelligence and her knowledge of his insecurities to smack him into submission -- or, at least, into silence. But Frank could feel the adrenaline coursing in his bloodstream, and his heart would pound. Like many Americans in the late 20th century, Audrey was divorced. Whatever her ex-husband's faults, had she used the same hit-and-run tactics on him?

# CHAPTER TWELVE

Predictably, Frank's meager savings were depleted in Washington before he could raise funds for the documentary, and he had to look for a job. He had hoped to get lucky, but – as they said in the Army – hope is not a plan. He assessed his marketable skills. He was a good writer, much better than most academics. Feelers to The Washington Post went unanswered, but The Washington Times gave him a tryout. This led to three years on the Foreign Desk.

After leaving The Washington Times, Frank spent more than a year trying to support himself as a free-lance writer. His most memorable rejection came from the editor of The Washington Post's Sunday Outlook section: "If you were Daniel Patrick Moynihan, we'd publish this in a minute," she said. "But you're not, so we won't." Frank admired the honesty.

On his fifth attempt to get a job at The Washington Post, Frank was hired by the Editorial Department. During his ten years at The Post, Frank noticed a pattern he never was able to decode. Some people, decidedly talented, were fast-tracked and given a series of increasingly desirable assignments. But others, in Frank's eyes equally talented, were dead-ended and never moved off square one. Of course, Frank was unaware of this pattern when he interviewed for the job.

"I think you'll find this opportunity opens many doors," his future boss said. The job was primarily editing, but she promised that he would be able to do some writing.

This did not prove to be the case. Frank was a copy editor for a decade, and in that time had only five or six essays published in the paper. In a meeting Frank requested with his boss to discuss his disappointment, she admitted, in so many words, that she had lied to him.

Frank met Janet in February of 1985 at a party at the home of one of The Washington Times editors. She had come with a boyfriend but spent most of the evening talking with Frank. She approached him at the buffet table, struck up a conversation, and asked all the right questions. She was tall and looked like a young Lauren Bacall, with the same kind of sexy, low-pitched voice. Her business was interior design and kitchen remodeling. She had lived several years in Paris, spoke very good French and not bad German. She was in the phone book.

He ran into her the following summer at a bakery near her Georgetown office. They both were happy to see each other.

"How's Dirk?" Frank inquired.

He tried to look suitably lugubrious when she said that they had broken up.

"Maybe we should get together some time," he offered.

But, as it turned out, she called first. Her friend Betsy was hosting an outdoor dinner party. Would he like to come?

"You're so *fatsoenlijk,*" she said on their third date, using a Dutch word she had picked up on buying trips to Amsterdam. Frank learned that *fatsoenlijk* meant decent, reliable, honest, straightforward, aboveboard, trustworthy, and dependable. And it was true. He was all those things. Moreover, she found him interesting, which was true as well. But, as he approached age 42, he had begun to accept the fact that he also was high-strung, gloomy, needy, self-shaming, judgmental, and hyper-reactive. Despite these faults, which he didn't hide, how wonderful it was to be appreciated by a woman who could discern his real virtues and place the greater value on them! Janet wasn't deluding herself or engaging in wishful thinking. In her eyes, his good qualities – his *fatsoenlijkheid* -- outweighed his shortcomings. At least for now. How lucky. He hoped it would last.

And for several years it did. Frank admired Janet's European ways and sophisticated taste. She, in turn, admired his integrity and his mind. He was grateful for the easy way they fell into bed, as natural as breathing, as if they had been making love for years. No drama, no preconditions, no jumping through hoops.

He moved into her townhouse in the spring of 1986. Red dogwood flowers floated down to cover his boxes in the rented trailer. His child support payments left him little disposable income, so she charged him only nominal rent. She saw him through a long period of unemployment between The Washington Times and The Washington Post. Once when he got food poisoning and was gushing fluid from both ends, he vomited helplessly as he sat on the toilet. She cleaned up after him.

The kids still were small when Sandy's manic depression forced her hospitalization, and Janet unhesitatingly agreed that Don and Laura should come to Washington. Janet acted as their stepmother for a semester, until Sandy could care for them again.

But Frank noticed a curious thing. Although Janet resembled Lauren Bacall, who was Jewish, and although her former boyfriend was Jewish, she didn't seem to like Jews much. He was shocked when she made mildly anti-Semitic remarks in front of Don and Laura. Frank didn't know French, but he told her immediately in schoolboy German never to talk that way in the presence of the children.

Frank couldn't figure it out. He had received only good from Jews, and as far as he knew the same was true of Janet. He was sure that no Jew had ever wronged her. If so, he would have heard about it -- repeatedly. Janet's words made him uneasy, but he decided not to make a big deal out of them. To do so would have been massively disruptive for both him and the children.

Frank retained a lawyer in Maryland. After a long and expensive process, his divorce from Sandy was finalized in the summer of 1987.

# CHAPTER THIRTEEN

When Frank went to work for The Washington Post in 1989, he considered himself a New Deal Democrat. Of course, he was more socially conservative than the average Post staffer, but he still thought of government as the best means for people to organize for the common good. Sink-or-swim social Darwinism held no allure. He believed in a safety net. He had benefitted from government programs – educational benefits under the GI bill and unemployment insurance, for example -- and he saw no reason why other such measures shouldn't be undertaken. He marveled at the enduring value of Depression-era improvements by the Works Progress Administration and the Civilian Conservation Corps. This was government in action, and the Democratic Party was the party of government.

But he began to lose confidence in the kind of people who embraced big government. Allowing for exceptions, they were arrogant, believing that smart people like them should be in charge. They basked in the glow of their moral superiority and felt the need to look down on the common run of humanity. They seemed more interested in grabbing and holding power than in helping the "little guy," for whom most had a profound aversion. As in the Soviet Union, where the "vanguard of the proletariat" shunned the proletariat, these "progressive" Americans abhorred rubbing elbows with the hoi polloi. They knew what was best for everyone, and they didn't mind marshaling the power of the state to enforce compliance with their preferences. They aggrandized power to confiscate wealth and redistribute it to their growing list of government-dependent constituencies, in which they fostered feelings of entitlement, resentment, and victimhood. To them the Constitution was not the supreme law of the land, but rather an obsolete document written by dead, white, slaveholding males that could be disregarded or reinterpreted at whim. And although they called themselves "liberals," they were anything but liberal. They were the most intolerant, rigid, and doctrinaire group of people Frank had ever encountered. They were in their element in Washington. And The Washington Post, second only to The New York Times, embodied their ethos.

The last straw came the day after the 1992 Georgia primary. Frank reasoned that he had no place in a political party in which a slacker like Bill Clinton could beat a Medal of Honor winner like Bob Kerrey in a southern state with a long martial tradition. Like all humans in a fallen world, Kerrey had his faults. But he was basically decent, even *fatsoenlijk*, and he had lost part of his leg in the service of his country. Clinton was slick and shifty: a hustler, a miscreant, a shirker, and a confidence man. He was as full of shit as a Christmas goose. A blind man could see that. The former Arkansas governor was not *fatsoenlijk*, no mistake. In fact, he lacked any trace of *fatsoenlijkheid*. But the staff of The Washington Post, along with the rest of the American news media, fell in love. Of course, they wouldn't admit it, even to themselves, but Frank could see that they were in the tank for Bill and Hillary Clinton. In ways great and small, but mostly small, they became Clinton shills.

For Frank this was the death of a thousand cuts. The faint discomfort he had felt at the newspaper was morphing into an active aversion. Frank either was unwilling to hide his feelings or was incapable of such guile. If pressed, he wouldn't have been able to say which.

"You don't have to die on every hill," his sister told him over the phone, "and you don't have to let people know you hate them. Remember 'The Godfather.' Keep your friends close and your enemies closer."

But although Frank had a Sicilian spleen, he lacked Sicilian cunning. Was he too Americanized? That couldn't be the explanation because his co-workers considered him a Kamikaze. His grandmother from Valledolmo, near Corleone, wouldn't have given herself away. A real Sicilian, recognizing his powerless and dependent state, wouldn't have tipped off his antagonists, thereby inviting their retaliation. His grandmother would have played dumb for decades, if necessary, to protect the interests of her family.

Or was it Frank's pride that made him reckless? Pride never was the whole explanation. Most often a matter of principle was involved.

In the summer of 1991 a motorcade conveying Rabbi Menachem Mendel Schneerson, then the Lubavitcher Rebbe, accidentally struck and killed a black child in the Crown Heights section of Brooklyn. Local blacks, incited by Al Sharpton, responded to the accident by rioting and attacking Jews, several of whom were seriously wounded. A mob surrounded and savagely murdered a 29-year-old Jewish doctoral student from Australia.

But the news media, beginning with the hometown New York Times, reported the violence as "racial strife," as if both sides were equally to blame. This infuriated Frank. Blacks were attacking Jews, not the other way around. Any reputable news organization should make this clear. To misreport such an outrage was irresponsible journalism.

Months later, Frank put the headline "Pogrom in Brooklyn" on a commentary piece written by the publisher's sister. His Jewish bosses -- Editorial Page Editor Beth Brenner and her deputy, Mike Feldblum – reviewed the page proofs and changed the headline to "A Crime in Brooklyn" but did not reprimand him. Trouble came when one of the editorial writers – a large, powerfully built black man known for his nasty temper – stormed into the tiny office the copy editors shared and demanded to know who had written the headline. Frank acknowledged his work. The man upbraided Frank for writing an inaccurate and inflammatory headline, then left the room.

Frank followed him into the hall. The headline was not inaccurate, Frank said.

An unpleasant face-off ensued. The editorial writer angrily told Frank that Mayor Dinkins personally had assured him that nothing like an anti-Jewish riot had taken place. Frank checked his impulse to say that Mayor Dinkins was a moron, an irresponsible bumbler unworthy of his office. Enough was enough. The attempt to intimidate him had failed. He would not obfuscate the facts. Washington Post management could do what it wanted. The newspaper was their sandbox. He was a wage slave for eight hours a day, but he made it clear to all concerned that his mind and his spirit were free.

Things slid downhill after Clinton got the nomination and even more with his subsequent inauguration. When friends called, Frank didn't hide his displeasure at working in a Clinton cheerleading section. At quitting time one night, after the others had left, a female copy editor tried to warn him.

"We don't like it when you talk like that," she said.

But Frank's state of mind wouldn't allow him to take heed. *He* wasn't the sycophant of some sleazy politician. *He* wasn't the flunky of a shameless swindler or the dupe of a bullshit artist. What did *he* have to be ashamed of?

"Did you get a dozen roses from Clinton for that wet kiss you gave him?" Frank asked one of the senior editorial writers one morning.

"Politics is binary, my boy," he replied, meaning the publisher and the editorial board favored Clinton over the elder Bush.

# CHAPTER FOURTEEN

Frank figured that since he was sidetracked at The Post, he might as well take advantage of what fringe benefits he could. And the most rewarding benefit for him was learning from the many fascinating experts of varied specialties who submitted essays to the op-ed page. He had to talk with them anyway in the course of editing their submissions. (Some required heavy editing, and some needed only minor stylistic adjustments.) Beth said he could do what he wanted as long as he made no mistakes and the author approved his changes.

Frank first would notify the writer by phone that the FAX was coming, and they would speak again after the author had reviewed the edited copy. What an intellectual feast! Frank had the chance to discuss a multitude of topics with the most knowledgeable sources.

Or so he thought.

Once, when he had Milton Friedman on the line, Frank took the opportunity to ask the great man a question about macroeconomics that had puzzled him for some time. It was not a hostile query, but it was a challenging one. Friedman was not at all offended, and he asked his wife, Rose, to pick up the extension because he wanted her input. Frank was delighted by the stimulating and rewarding three-way discussion.

But an envious copy editor, the same woman who had admonished Frank, complained to the boss. Surely eminent luminaries, some of them Nobel laureates like Friedman, didn't submit their analyses to The Washington Post to be challenged by Frank DiRaimo. Beth Brenner, known for her North Korean management style, heartily agreed. Beth strictly forbad Frank from engaging in any personal discussion with the contributors.

In January of 1992, an acquaintance of Frank's, Amos Perlmutter, a political scientist at American University, published a prescient essay in The Washington Post titled "Wishful Thinking About Islamic Fundamentalism." Almost ten years before the attacks of September 11, 2001, Perlmutter warned: "Islamic fundamentalism is an aggressive revolutionary movement as militant and violent as the Bolshevik, Fascist, and Nazi movements of the past." He wrote that by its very nature Islamic fundamentalism is "authoritarian, anti-democratic, anti-secular" and can't be reconciled with the "Christian-secular universe." Perlmutter argued that to thwart the movement's goal of establishing a "totalitarian Islamic state" in the Middle East, the United States should ensure that Islamic fundamentalism is "stifled at birth."

Sophisticates denounced Perlmutter as a "racist" and a confrontational alarmist desperate for an external enemy to replace the Soviet Union after the end of the Cold War. When the professor telephoned to discuss the possibility of rebutting his critics, Frank took the call.

"I knew you'd fight back," Frank said.

An office fink reported these five words to Beth. Frank's defense -- that he had a life before he came to The Washington Post, and he had a right to talk to his friends -- did no good. He was suspended without pay for three days. That month it was tough to make both the child support payment and his contribution to Janet's mortgage, which had increased with his job at The Post.

The mother of one of the U.S. Army Rangers killed in Mogadishu in October of 1993 wrote a letter to the editor highly critical of President Clinton for not providing adequate security backup for U.S. forces in Somalia. Frank noticed that the letters editor kept putting it to the bottom of the pile. Frank waited until the letters editor went on vacation and then published the heartfelt missive. The letters editor was furious with Frank upon her return and remained so for weeks.

# CHAPTER FIFTEEN

Of all the institutions Frank had experienced, including the Catholic Church and the U.S. Army, The Washington Post was by far the most hierarchical. Never mind the false familiarity of addressing bosses by their first names. Frank had been freer to express himself in the military than he was at the newspaper.

The Post also was the most sexually sterile environment he ever had been in, although it had its share of attractive women. Frank, being Frank, pushed back against this too.

"The Washington Times is a rabbit hutch compared to this place," he complained to a male colleague." To others, he referred to a pretty Peruvian photographer as "Cupcake del Mundo." And he would direct the editorial aides to take potentially libelous letters to the 9th floor for review. "Run this by sweet Mary Jane," he would say. "You know. The lawyer with the nice legs."

This resulted in the envious female copy editor filing a sexual harassment complaint against him for creating a "hostile work environment." Frank was exonerated after a lengthy investigation, but the experience was terrifying, and it had the chilling and demoralizing effect the woman intended.

Of all the stuffed shirts at The Washington Post, the deracinated Ivy League Jews annoyed him most. They submerged whatever residual *Yiddishkeit* they might still have possessed in the quest for a not quite convincing impersonation of old-time establishment WASPs.

Mike Feldblum was the Editorial Department's resident expert on national security and foreign affairs, subjects of particular interest to Frank. It seemed to Frank that Mike calibrated his editorials by zeroing in on the conventional wisdom and then adjusting his sights one click to the left. Mike's editorials on the Middle East were masterpieces of equivocation: On the one hand, on the other hand. If Israel would do this, then its enemies might do that. Mike seemed reluctant to engage in a full-throated defense of the Jewish state, something The Washington Times's Wes Pruden – who wasn't Jewish – routinely did. Was Mike ashamed? Ethnically insecure? He seemed to dread being seen as a man of tribal loyalties. Rather, he cultivated the persona of a sophisticated, detached analyst – cool, above the fray, and oh-so-capable of nuance.

Columnist Richard Cohen traveled to Germany and reported on the resurgence Jewish life there after the end of the Cold War. Cohen sent back a column that Frank titled "Shabbos in Berlin." Mike changed the headline to "Sabbath in Berlin," an evasion Frank thought timorous and unnecessarily confusing to the reader. Whose sabbath? The Seventh-day

Adventists'? The Christian Sabbath? Friday prayers at the mosque? The Wiccan Wheel of the Year? Readers unfamiliar with the Yiddish word would quickly grasp its meaning from the text. Frank remembered that Mike, in an unguarded moment, had revealed that he didn't want people to think "those Jews" were running the show at The Washington Post.

Yet, if one disregarded a trace of primness and a slight pompousness, there was something appealing about Mike. Tall, black-haired, and handsome, athletic and youthful despite his years, he had a good sense of humor when he deigned to display it and sound leadership instincts he wasn't always willing to employ. He had served in the Marine Corps in the early 1950s. By all indications, he was a devoted husband and father. Frank wanted to like Mike. And, if Frank could have admitted it to himself, he wanted Mike to like him.

Frank really didn't know what to expect the first time he wished Mike a "Gut Shabbos" as the older man was leaving the office one Friday evening. He sincerely wanted Mike to have a good Sabbath if Mike observed it, and even if he didn't. Although a hint of mischief lurked in Frank's words, he was not looking for trouble and was hoping that Mike would respond warmly. Wasn't it clear Frank was trying to establish a human connection? Didn't Frank's familiarity with the language and customs of European Jewry count for something?

Mike stiffened. With a grim expression, he looked away, quickened his pace, and walked wordlessly out the door.

So that's the way it is, Frank thought when the confusion and hurt subsided. If you belong to an exclusive club, you don't want an interloper suddenly to come along wearing your colors and pumping your arm with the secret handshake. But after Frank had time to reflect, he decided that wasn't the

full explanation for Mike's coldness – or even the most important part of it. A horrifying thought obtruded. Could Mike
have assumed that Frank had taunted him for being Jewish?
Unlikely. And if Mike was crazy enough to believe that, it was
his problem.

Frank examined his conscience and realized that he had,
in fact, gently taunted Mike – not for being Jewish, but rather
for not being Jewish enough. In the weeks following Mike's
snub, Frank's comprehension grew. He wished he could talk
the matter over with Janet, but she wouldn't get it, and it would
only upset her. Instead of receiving the emotional support he
craved, she would attack him. He rehearsed an imaginary dia-
tribe he knew he never would deliver:

"*Nu*, Mr. Fancy-Schmantzy. It's understood that you went to
Harvard and all that, but I know who you are and where you came
from. Where's your *Yiddishkeit*? Your father from Russia -- the hab-
erdasher with the funny accent -- to *him* I could have wished a 'Gut
Shabbos.' *He* would have liked it, even if he was my boss. Even if
I swept his floors. Even if I delivered his coal or hauled the ashes
from his furnace. Are you better than your father? Who the fuck
do you think you are?"

Beth was like a hurricane, a force of nature. She couldn't
help who she was, but Mike had to work at being a dickhead.

# CHAPTER SIXTEEN

Frank's unhappiness at work took its toll on his relationship with Janet. "Tell me about your day," she would say. Frank would think back on the day: the pages he had worked on, the editing and formatting he had done, the column widths, the layouts, the effort to get the indents to line up on both sides of the illustrations he had chosen, the point size of the headlines, the dummy outlines, measuring with the pica ruler, kerning the type to force a fit, dealing with the snits of temperamental unionized printers – not a few of them deaf mutes – whose cooperation he needed but over whom he had no authority, the proof sheets, making the fixes, checking the fixes, begging harried news editors for updates to ensure that the next day's editorials were not risibly overtaken by events, keeping a death watch over Herblock so if the octogenarian cartoonist expired at his easel the hole on the page could be filled, the phone calls to the contributors, which by now were perfunctory.

"I don't want to hear about *that!*" Janet would say. "I want to hear about your *day.*"

So Frank would tell her about his interactions with people, which usually were distasteful and disappointing. This made Janet even angrier and more exasperated with him. He felt judged, criticized, and rejected. Why did she have to ask? Wasn't it enough that he bore his lot stoically? Didn't he show up for work five days a week? What did she want from him? He was as *fatsoenlijk* as ever, but this seemed to count for little with her now.

Janet resented it that Frank spent so much time in the morning reading the newspaper. "Beth Brenner pays me to know what's in this paper," he said, accurately enough. But winning an argument with Janet would have been like winning an argument with Beth. His logic might be impeccable, and all the facts could be in his favor, but the cost was so high he'd lose anyway.

Their social life suffered. When they were out among people, Frank inevitably would be asked what he did. "I'm a newspaper employee," he would reply bitterly, without elaborating. This would make others uncomfortable, and some, not knowing how to respond, laughed nervously. Janet would be annoyed at him and embarrassed for him.

The discontent carried over into the bedroom. Although in his sixth decade, Frank had not yet learned that "I'm miserable, and it's your job to make me feel better by having sex with me," is not an approach that women find erotic – even as an unstated assumption. He would learn later that no woman wants that job and that it was unfair and unrealistic for him to assign it to Janet. Had he understood, he would have been just as horny and needy, but he would have been softer and more solicitous.

In the Spring of 1996, after ten years of living together, Frank moved out of Janet's townhouse. His tiny basement-level "garden apartment" was lonely and cramped, but it was better than the constant tension and the feeling that he was disappointing her. They remained friends, staying in phone contact, getting together once or twice a week, having dinner, seeing the occasional movie. They picked each other up at the airport. They drove each other back from their colonoscopies. They still had sex, and sometimes it was very good, but it was hit and miss. The next year followed the last.

It wasn't all bad. Frank enjoyed the company of the irascible J.Y. Smith, whom he had replaced in the Editorial Department. Like Frank, Joe Smith was a truth-teller, which had caused him trouble at The Post. The growing tension between him and Mike Feldblum made Smith eager to return to the Obituary Desk. And Frank shared many laughs with feature writer Henry Allen, a quirky genius who would go on to win a Pulitzer Prize for criticism. Both Smith and Allen were Marine Corps veterans. Smith had seen heavy combat in Korea, and Allen had served in Vietnam.

Frank became friendly with columnist Bill Raspberry -- although they disagreed about same-sex "marriage," which Frank considered a contradiction in terms. As a sign of respect, Frank sometimes would address the older man as *Don Guglielmo*. On the day Raspberry's Pulitzer Prize for commentary was announced, the columnist credited Frank, in front of others, for giving him some of his best ideas. This was extravagant and unexpected praise, and Frank wasn't sure there was any truth to it, but it showed what a classy guy Raspberry was.

Raspberry, however, thought Frank too hot-headed for his own good and gently tried to steer him toward the smoother path. Richard Cohen, too, counseled Frank not to be so quick to reveal himself – to play his cards closer to the chest.

But Frank never could resist the opportunity to make a point, especially if it exposed an overlooked truth. George McGovern published an essay on the op-ed page, and somehow his home state was misidentified in the tag line, which read, in italics: "The writer, the Democratic Party's nominee for president in 1972, is a former senator from North Dakota." Except it was South Dakota!

In the Editorial Department, the knives were out. Who would Beth punish for this? All the copy editors had missed the error on the proof sheet, but who had introduced it electronically? Had a careless printer in the composing room mistyped it from the paper manuscript? Or, much worse, had a copy editor blundered? Keystrokes left tracks, and it was possible to review the history directory. Computers didn't lie. Someone would pay.

The crisis was defused by McGovern's generous response. He simply refused to make a big deal of it. "It's OK," he said to Frank when Frank telephoned to apologize. McGovern's voice carried a trace of sadness but no rancor. McGovern would have been justified in raising hell. And if he had, Beth would have been merciless.

What a wonderful guy! Frank thought gratefully. If Frank had been the author, he'd have made his displeasure known. After all, people should do their jobs. And how would Richard Nixon have reacted in McGovern's place?

But we don't pay presidents to be nice guys, Frank thought. He was pretty sure that Mike was pleased with himself for having supported McGovern in 1972.

"Did you ever think about the outcome of the Yom Kippur War if McGovern had been elected?" Frank asked Mike. "That massive airlift Nixon ordered to resupply Israel? The chances of McGovern doing that are just about zero."

Mike's eyes widened. Frank interpreted the look on the Mike's face to mean that Mike had not, in fact, considered that contingency. Nixon was a bogeyman to senior Washington Post staffers, who took pride in the newspaper's role in deposing the president during Watergate. Frank was using a cattle prod on a sacred cow.

# CHAPTER SEVENTEEN

"Do you often feel you have five things going on, and you can't keep track of any of them?" Dr. Hartman asked.

"Yes," Frank said.

"That's my most diagnostic question," the psychiatrist said with a smile. "Someone who didn't have ADD wouldn't even understand what I was asking."

It had been a long consultation, and Frank had been forced to excuse himself twice to urinate. Perhaps he'd been keyed up. He'd suspected that he had attention deficit disorder since he first read about the condition years ago. He was not the suggestible type, nor was he a hypochondriac. On the contrary. Frank used to read his father's medical journals for their sheer interest. He'd learned about myriad diseases, infirmities, pathologies, maladies, afflictions, and indispositions -- both the exotic and the commonplace – and he never imagined that he suffered from any of them. But the lengthy article in The New York Times Sunday magazine had hit him like a ton of bricks. ADD? He was a textbook case.

"The comorbidity of ADD and depression is very high," Dr. Hartman said. "It's not surprising. Most ADD people are smart – in your case, very smart – but all their lives others castigate them for underperforming. They internalize those harsh judgments and become their own worst critics. They offend people without meaning to, and they have trouble with relationships and bosses. Some rack up failure after failure. Others, like you, have managed to compensate fairly well. But even the skilled compensators tend to lead lives of chronic frustration and self-doubt, as you've indicated to me."

"Yes," Frank said.

Did the doctor's words justify the hope, finally, for proper treatment, or did they mandate despair? Hartman was an eminent physician, internationally known for his expertise, and it was obvious to Frank that the doctor knew a lot more general medicine than most psychiatrists. And Hartman wasn't just a prescription-writer. He prided himself on his psychotherapy, a skill set that was becoming harder to find among MDs.

"I'm going to treat your depression first because the stimulant medicine for ADD can make untreated depression worse." The psychiatrist noted the look on his patient's face.

"Don't worry. ADD isn't all bad. I'd say 50 percent of the symptoms are positive."

"Really?"

"Sure. ADD people are often creative, intuitive, and – as I've said – highly intelligent. They're capable of independent thinking, They're debunkers and truth-tellers. Many have a spirit of adventure. They tend to be mavericks, which is OK to a point. When they're engaged, they have a lot of energy – especially the hyperactive ones, which you're not, but even those without hyperactivity can be tenacious, sometimes to the point of stubbornness. If they're not engaged, ADD people tend to lose interest easily, and they dissipate their energies flitting from one thing to another.

"But getting back to the positives: Although their distractibility and scattered thoughts can cause their partners to see them as cold, indifferent, and detached, in my experience they tend to be generous, forgiving, and soft-hearted. That gets overlooked with all the hammering they take."

Dr. Hartman paused for a moment and regarded Frank kindly. "And remember, while you might overlook the obvious and miss what others see, you're also capable of seeing what others miss. That's worth a lot."

⋙ ⋘

Over the next few years, Frank tried every antidepressant the doctor prescribed. None helped much, and all had side effects he was unwilling to endure. One even produced heart palpitations. And although he at first got good results from very small doses of stimulants, his body quickly built up a resistance. Then anything approaching a therapeutic dose raised his blood pressure to dangerous levels, interfered with sleep, and killed his appetite. By the turn of the 21st century, he had taken himself off all psychotropic medications. He felt better physically, if nothing else.

Frank recognized ADD in the character of Erlend Nikulausson, the flawed husband in one of his favorite novels, Sigrid Undset's *Kristin Lavransdatter* trilogy. He knew he was supposed to disapprove of Erlend – strongly! -- but he found the medieval Norwegian knight appealing, even endearing. Despite Erlend's manifest faults, Frank admired his independence, his irreverence, his open-hearted courage, and his nobility of spirit. Erlend wasn't petty or niggling, unlike the piss-ant backstabbers and sedulous strivers Frank had to deal with in Washington. Frank wished he had a friend like Erlend, and he wished he could be such a friend to himself.

# CHAPTER EIGHTEEN

For most of the 1990s, Frank didn't know what to make of the wars that ravaged the Balkans after the breakup of Yugoslavia. At first he accepted the received wisdom that it was all the fault of the Serbs. But as the decade approached its end, he came to believe this was unfair and inaccurate. By the Spring of 1999 -- when lapsed peacenik Bill Clinton and his secretary of state, Madeleine "The Merciless" Albright, decided to bomb the Serbian people into submission for the benefit of a Muslim drug gang -- Frank was incensed. But the bleeding hearts at The Post, including many of those who had condemned Vietnam as an "immoral" war, had no compassion for the Serbs. It drove Frank crazy to know that *his* Air Force, funded by *his* tax dollars, was blowing Serb babies to bits.

Frank tried to describe a B-52 strike to one of his younger colleagues. In Vietnam he had found them terrifying, even though they were intended to keep him alive rather than to kill him. First, the stillness. The bombers flew so high as to make no sound. Then, out of nowhere, volcanic explosions. The earth would erupt, the ground would quake, and great waves of orange fire would ascend to the heavens. What could live under such a bombardment? And this, Frank said, was what our own government was doing to a civilian population in the heart of Europe.

The younger man's efforts to keep an impassive face betrayed his fear. He stayed silent. Was Frank trying to recruit him into his Kamikaze squadron? No thanks. He had a little girl to support.

"How does it feel to be outsmarted by Albanians?" Frank asked Mike. From Mike's face, Frank saw he had struck home. Frank knew it could cost him, but he didn't care.

Beth died toward the end of the bombing campaign. She had fought cancer courageously for a long time. She never seemed to like Frank, although she had hired him a decade earlier and could have gotten rid of him whenever she wished. Beth was a control freak, and she knew that Frank never would be fully under her control. She was a remarkable woman – scary brilliant, ultra-competent, and ruthless. Her turn of phrase, written or aural, could make the angels sing. In ten years, he had never seen her make a bad edit. She made edits he disliked that advanced her personal and political agendas, but those were shrewd and calculated choices. She never acted out of ineptitude. She was a dazzling, world-class, twice-in-a-century talent, which was one of the reasons he hadn't quit.

There were two schools of thought about Beth, whom the newspaper's art critic referred to as "the tiny terror." Majority opinion held that marriage and children would have mellowed her, but Frank believed it was one of God's mercies that Beth had remained single and childless. He thought she would have been a disaster as a wife and a worse mother. He couldn't imagine any man married to her, and children – especially sons – would have been doomed.

As Beth lay dying in her home, Frank wondered if he should pay her a visit. The Catholic Church had taught him that visiting the sick was one of the Corporal Works of Mercy. And wasn't it a mitzvah – a commandment, or good deed – in the Jewish faith? Beth lived around the corner, only a few blocks away. Frank had been a cafeteria Catholic, picking and choosing as he liked, but he could find no objection to this precept. Indeed, it seemed sinful to ignore it.

The tiny Guatemalan caregiver greeted him effusively at the door. "Oh, *señor*," she said, drawing her hands together as if in prayer, "it's so good you are here." She praised Frank as a righteous man and guided him to Beth's deathbed.

"Hello, Beth," Frank said.

Beth, wracked by the disease and the treatments that no longer kept her alive, was repulsed by his presence. Angry and disgusted, she averted her eyes, refusing even to look in his direction. Silence hung in the air.

Frank wanted to bolt, but he was afraid an instantaneous exit would alarm the caregiver. He hurt in the core of his being. Never had he been in such psychic pain. It was one of the worst moments of his life. After a decent interval, he spoke.

"You're tough, Beth. I've always admired you for that."

She grunted as if to say, "You got that right."

Frank turned and made his exit, nodding to the Guatemalan woman as he passed through the foyer.

Beth died shortly after. That day Frank drove to work but had no recollection of doing so. He walked home, trying to burn off adrenaline, and he took the bus to work the following morning. After a few days, Frank went to the place near his apartment where he normally parked his car. It wasn't there. He couldn't figure it out. From his desk at The Post, he reported the vehicle stolen to the D.C. Metropolitan Police. They had no knowledge of it. Days more passed. Frank almost gave the car up for lost, but then decided to check the streets in the neighborhood of the newspaper. There it was, just as he'd left it. He didn't even have a ticket.

Frank remembered that he had done the same thing more than 35 years earlier. On November 22, 1963, Frank returned to his parents' home after a day of college and rested in his room for a few minutes before reporting for work at the drugstore. His mother came charging up the stairs, terror in her eyes. He had never seen her move so fast.

"The president's been shot!" she said.

Frank drove to the pharmacy in daze. There, on the radio, he learned that President Kennedy had been killed. With all the craziness of the next few days, including Jack Ruby's killing of Lee Harvey Oswald on live television, nobody noticed at first that Frank's mother's station wagon was missing. When its absence was noted, Frank had no knowledge of its whereabouts. Finally, Frank and his mother searched the streets around the pharmacy in his father's Pontiac. There it was.

The shame and hurt of Beth's final rejection lingered for months. It buzzed in his head, knotted his neck and shoulders, and hung heavy in his gut. At unexpected moments, his scalp would sweat. He wished he could embrace the narrative of Beth, bitchy to the end, behaving inexcusably. But something about that was too easy, too self-exculpatory and unfair to Beth. What was he missing? Slowly, it came to him, and he arrived at an internal dialogue:

"Corporal Works of Mercy, my ass. What were you really looking for when you went over there? Was it to give or to get? Did you have any reason to expect she'd be happy to see a sullen, insubordinate employee? You were trying to exploit her weakened condition and turn her feeble physical state to your advantage. You hoped that surely, on her deathbed, about to meet her Maker, she finally would show you some of the affection, appreciation, and approval you'd always wanted from her. Beth could see right through you. She knew you better than you know yourself. She was under no obligation to like you and had every right to resent your shameless attempt to manipulate her, which simply validated her low opinion of you. You intruded. You violated her privacy and disturbed her tranquility on one of her last days on Earth."

Then, finally: "Good for you, Beth. Way to go. May you rest in peace."

Frank had read in self-help books that mentally healthy people are indifferent to external validation and therefore don't seek it from others. Horseballs, he thought. What normal person wouldn't want the approval of his boss? Not that he required it. He'd functioned without it for ten years, hadn't he?

A parallel conceit was the New Age nonsense about not needing material resources for a good life. Tell that to the landlord. Tell that to the supermarket cashier. When Frank returned to grad school in 1979, a fellow student had said to him: "I've been broke on $8,000 a year, and I've been broke on $80,000 a year. Being broke on 80K is better." Frank had been treated well, and he'd been treated badly. Being treated well was better.

Mike Feldblum, nearing retirement, was named interim Editorial Page editor, and Alan Solway, one of the younger editorial writers and a former foreign correspondent, was tapped to replace Beth. At first it seemed to Frank that peace finally had come to the Editorial Department, and perhaps he could spend the rest of his working life at The Post. The constant tension imposed by Beth's tyranny dissipated. Beth had operated under the principle of divide and rule, so she had encouraged jealousy, backbiting and tale-telling among the copy editors. She had shown favoritism among the editorial writers, with predictable results. After her death, such viciousness subsided. Mike could be reasoned with, and Alan was congenial. Life was good.

# CHAPTER NINETEEN

B ut as the months went on, Frank could sense that something was amiss. Mike's demeanor toward Frank became steadily more crisp and brisk. And in many subtle ways, Alan conveyed the message that he no longer was a working stiff – a dues-paying member of the Washington-Baltimore Newspaper Guild, Local 32035 -- but rather had become a vigilant mandarin of Washington Post management. Frank reluctantly drew the conclusion that he was under the gun, targeted for removal. They were waiting for him to mess up.

Armed with this insight, Frank tried to be especially meticulous in the execution of his duties. His performance had to be flawless. He wanted to leave The Post under his own steam at the time of his choosing. He never had been fired from anything, and he didn't want this to be the first time.

But, paradoxically, the better Frank understood that they were out to get him, the more error-prone he became. His nervousness, and the effort to hide it, drained and distracted him and interfered with his effective functioning. Being a copy editor was like being a Secret Service agent: all defense, no offense. You could forestall 200 assassinations and prevent six, but the one that gets by destroys you.

One night as Alan was leaving the building, he instructed Frank to make a change to one of the editorials. Frank assured Alan that it would be done, and Alan went home. But just then an op-ed contributor called in a panic. Congress had taken action late in the day that made a revision to his essay imperative. The page already was pasted up and ready to go. Frank sent an editorial aide to the composing room to mark through the column with yellow crayon and to tell the printers to hold the page. Frank worked with the writer over the phone to revise the affected paragraphs, and he had a colleague read behind him for accuracy. He checked the fit and found that a few lines now popped out of the formatted space.

He searched the text for opportunities to impose shorter constructions. His mind and fingers worked efficiently: Passive to active voice. Expunge "very" wherever it appears. Eliminate adverbs. Recast sentences that begin "there is" or "there are," or "it is" with the relentless sequence of subject-verb-object. Discard extraneous "that"s. Kern in those widows. Cheat on the space between lines. He re-justified and found he had a fit. Then he dropped the new type, descended to the composing room, and made sure the revised version was pasted up. He released the page, taking satisfaction in a job well done.

But he forgot to make Alan's fix.

Frank burned with shame the next day when Alan confronted him with his error. There was no excuse. He would have to try even harder.

Not long after, Frank again was on duty at night as deadline approached and Mike called from home to make a change to an editorial. Nothing was unusual about the call, nor in Mike's language. A transcript would have revealed no hostility. But Frank could hear an edge in Mike's voice, and the pacing of his words suggested menace. Frank had worked with Mike for more than ten years and knew the man's ways. This was different. Frank wasn't imagining things.

Frank called up the specified editorial on the computer screen. Mike spoke a name.

"Do you see it?" Mike asked.

Frank scanned the text.

"Yes, I've got it."

Mike dictated the change, which added background. Frank typed in the fix, checked for a fit, and then clicked the tab that sent the editorial to the composing room.

The next day Frank realized that the name had appeared twice in the editorial. Mike, reasonably enough, had intended the identifying information to follow the first reference. Frank had made the change to the second reference. Mike made his displeasure clear.

Frank was relieved that he had some vacation coming. He needed a break. This time he would stay in town. His last two trips to Minnesota had been unpleasant, even painful. As Sandy's health deteriorated, she had become violent. Once, as he was pulling into the driveway with Don and Laura, she started swinging at him through the open window of a rental car. The last time she was craftier. She said she had to speak to him privately about something very important. They went into Don's room, closed the door, and she attacked him. The kids would have to visit him in Washington. Maybe Christmas.

He spent his two weeks off annotating the diary of an obscure Scottish immigrant that provided a fascinating first-hand account of the United States in the 1830s. Frank had stumbled upon the document in a used bookstore and hoped he could get a university press to republish his annotated version. His footnotes explained the many arcane references modern readers would be unlikely to understand. He hoped things had blown over at The Post and that he would return to a bit of a fresh start. But he really didn't know what to expect.

It was like walking into an ambush. Frank barely was at his desk before Alan summoned him to Beth's office. It was in the process of becoming Alan's office, but the transition was incomplete. Some of Beth's books still were scattered on the shelves, and the furniture was in disarray. Suddenly, Frank missed Beth.

Alan was all business and wasted no time. Frank's services no longer were required. Alan looked uncomfortable but determined, like a young Mafioso sent on his first hit. Frank almost felt sorry for him.

He also almost felt sorry for Mike, who Frank was pretty sure had made the decision to fire him. Frank concluded that Mike was plagued by the insecurity Frank had seen in other successful children of immigrants. Until the European genocide, Mike's father could have returned to the Pale of Settlement and be reunited with people just like him. Lacking such an anchor, the earnest strivers of the second generation had to construct an American identity from scratch. They felt an interminable need to prove themselves, they took themselves very seriously, and they were easily rattled by wild cards like Frank. To Mike, the genteel Eastern Establishment progressivism of The Washington Post was the epitome of respectability. His name on the masthead was testimony that he'd arrived. He had made it to the lifeboat, and he didn't want anyone rocking it. But even understanding all this, Frank thought Mike had shown himself to be petty. Other people had overcome bigger challenges than Mike's without losing their generosity of spirit.

Frank assumed he would have the rest of the day to set his affairs in order and to print some documents from his computer files. Not so. He was to leave immediately, and his computer access had been terminated during his absence. He no longer existed at The Washington Post. It was almost as if he had never existed. He thought of the Soviet Politburo, where the images of purged apparatchiks were erased from official photos.

Frank packed his reference books and personal effects into two cardboard boxes. A younger colleague helped him carry his stuff to 15th Street, where he would catch a cab home. On the elevator the man confirmed that it was Mike who was behind his dismissal.

During the next week, Frank signed many documents. To receive his modest severance, he was forced to promise never again to seek employment with The Washington Post Company. A company vice president with whom Frank was on friendly terms told him that Alan had said Frank was too smart to be a copy editor and should be writing his own stuff. Fair enough. But why, then, couldn't a place have been found for him in the vast Washington Post empire? On the Foreign Desk, for example, or in Newsweek magazine, or on one of the local papers, or in one of the television stations? Instead, he had to vow never to darken their door again.

But in a way, the question was moot. A part of him was relieved it was over. He had been dying at The Post. Maybe he should have quit long ago, even if he had nothing else lined up, although his next boss could have been as difficult as Beth with 20 percent of the brains and talent. Now *that* would have been intolerable.

Beth. Now he was sure of what he had long suspected. She knew he was overqualified and had kept him on because he brought depth and knowledge to her operations. He had been a valuable resource, a good backstop. She must have had a certain respect for him, even if it was purely utilitarian. For Beth, the quality of the product trumped personal antipathy. It was otherwise with Mike and Alan. In the months following his dismissal, Frank took grim satisfaction in the spike in corrections and "clarifications" that appeared on the editorial pages.

In time Frank came to understand what had kept him in Beth's Editorial Department. Words from his Psyche 101 class reverberated in his head. "Intermittent reinforcement is the most addictive kind." It's what keeps the rats hitting the lever for a pellet of food, it's what keeps the suckers coming back to the casinos, and it's what keeps people stuck in abusive relationships.

For it wasn't true that Beth *never* treated Frank with respect and appreciation. Occasionally, she would ask for his evaluation of an op-ed submission. If an essay had been scheduled for the page that Frank thought was particularly weak, she would take his opinion seriously.

Sometimes he would drop off papers on her desk and find her in a chatty mood. Usually, she would want to discuss the book she was reading, most often history or political biography. The editorial writers were on deadline, and she knew Frank was the one copy editor who could keep up with her. Because of her small size, she would make large books easier to handle by tearing them along the spine, reading one half at a time. On these occasions, she was almost girlish in her enthusiasm. She spoke to Frank not only as an equal, but also as a valued collaborator. During these discussions, Frank felt intimacy, warmth, and real human connection with Beth – as well as acute, delicious intellectual stimulation. It was just what he craved and just what he had been seeking when he took the job. It was intermittent reinforcement, and it had kept him hooked.

It took time to land on his feet. The Internet still was a novelty, and dial-up connections were slow. Frank's favorite pastimes had been browsing through libraries and poking around bookstores. Now more information than he ever could absorb was sitting in a box on his desk. Sometimes he would begin reading at night and be surprised by the dawn. Frank knew that had to stop, and he became more diligent in his job search. One day, on Connecticut Avenue, he ran into an acquaintance from the Foreign Desk of The Washington Times who had secured a good position at Consolidated Press. After the usual stutter-steps, he was hired. Thus began a process that led him, in the month of May in the year of grace 2000, to be standing in the State Department cafeteria with a tray of spaghetti in his hands.

# PART THREE

# CHAPTER TWENTY

Frank threaded his way among the tables and paused to survey the expanse. In a way, he was relieved he didn't see anyone he recognized. That simplified things. He didn't have to worry about whether he knew this person or that person well enough to ask to sit down, or if they would be offended if he didn't, or to decode from a distance signs of a private conversation. He hated to guess whether his presence would be welcomed or endured. He didn't need the agitation, especially when he was trying to eat.

A man jumped up from a nearby table, looked at his watch, bade farewell to his lunch companion, and hurried off. Left sitting before a half-eaten meal was Morris Gordon of the Associated Press and Frank's nominal counterpart. But that was a joke. Gordon had decades of experience at the job both in print and in radio, while Frank was a rank novice. Frank had a horror of untoward familiarity and of pushing himself where he wasn't wanted. Nevertheless, opportunities were seized or lost. Frank recalled that Admiral Arleigh Burke had been asked to explain the difference between an outstanding officer and a mediocrity: "About ten seconds," the admiral had said.

"Mr. Gordon, may I join you?"

Gordon looked up, surprised.

"Sure," he said flatly after a slight hesitation.

Having watched Gordon in action, Frank had concluded that the AP reporter was a traditional liberal but not a leftist. More important, Gordon was old enough to belong to a generation in which being a liberal and being a stalwart supporter of Israel were not mutually exclusive. A BBC man, not knowing Frank's sympathies, had mocked Gordon to Frank as a Zionist stooge, which only raised Gordon's standing in Frank's eyes.

"As you might know, I'm new at this, and the Middle East is a mysterious place to figure out."

Gordon looked at Frank with new interest.

"This Oslo thing has got me baffled," Frank said, twisting his spaghetti on his fork. He wondered if it was possible to eat the meal without spattering his shirt or tie. He recalled his father eating his pasta with a dishcloth tucked into the top of his shirt, and Frank wished he could do the same. It would be difficult to eat neatly and talk at the same time.

"How so?" asked Gordon.

"I know Oslo is supposed to be like the second coming of Christ, but I just can't see what the Israelis have got out of it – or what they can hope to get in the future. Terror attacks went way up after the 'peace' agreement, right?"

"Absolutely."

"And the Israelis brought the PLO back from Tunis, right?"

"Yes."

"Back from the dead. A miracle!"

Gordon looked narrowly at Frank.

"Tunis is a long way from Israel," Frank continued.

"Correct."

"And gave them guns! Guns that were turned against Israelis when Netanyahu opened that tunnel in Jerusalem a few years back."

Gordon leaned back in his chair and took an audible breath.

"And in a few months," Frank went on, "the lion is supposed to lie down with the lamb. The seven years of 'confidence building' between the two sides is scheduled to come to fruition. But I have no confidence! Check that. I'm confident that if a deal doesn't materialize, Israel will be blamed. And I'm confident there won't be a deal, because the Arabs will demand more than any Israeli government can grant. Even a Labor government. Even this one."

Frank put his napkin on his lap, took a sip of water, and pressed on.

"I thought Israel won its wars. Why must the winner sue for peace? Doesn't the victor impose the terms? What did Rabin think he was doing?"

Frank put a forkful of spaghetti in his mouth. It was getting cold but still tasted good. By now he was hungry. He looked at Gordon, chewing, waiting for his response.

"You've given this some thought," Gordon said.

"I'm trying to learn."

"And from me, you want?"

The sudden appearance of Yiddish word order almost made Frank smile.

"Your take. My grandmother wouldn't have painted herself into a corner like this. It's a sucker's game. I thought Jews were smart."

Surprise flickered on Gordon's face at Frank's violation of the taboo. "You're as blunt as an Israeli. Have you ever been there?"

"No."

"Maybe soon. Look, to answer your question, Israelis are brash but insecure. They have the virtues and vices of children. Inside, they're desperate for the world to love them. And the Ashkenazi elite." He paused. "Do you know --?"

"-- I know from Ashkenazim."

"OK. The Ashkenazi elite *really* wants to be loved by Europe."

"But that's crazy. Europe was a grave to their grandparents."

"I know. But despite everything, their grandparents were in love with Europe, especially Central and Western Europe. But Europe wasn't in love with them. Strictly one-way. It was unrequited then, and it's unrequited now. But the need for love is powerful, like an addiction."

"I think I see where you're going with this," Frank said.

"Zionism is Jewish nationalism, and Israel is a barracks state, but Europe has entered a post-national, pacifistic phase. Whether it will last, I don't know. The Europeans will tell you they've learned from harsh experience that war solves nothing. They put their confidence in international organizations like the United Nations and the World Court. But without war or the credible threat of war, Israel wouldn't last a week.

"So what these insecure, love-starved Israelis hear all the time is this: 'Why can't you make peace with your neighbors? Just give them something! We don't want high oil prices because of you. We don't want to be dragged into your quarrels. We don't want bombs going off in our cafés. You people cause trouble wherever you go. Have you Jews learned nothing? You're doing the same thing to the Palestinians that the Nazis did to you. We don't like your nationalism, and we recoil at your reliance on your army. Violence just begets more violence. Learn to be like us, or you'll be without a friend in the world. Even America will grow tired of you. You think you have problems now? You don't know what problems are. You'll be a pariah state worse than South Africa.' "

"That's why the Israelis imposed Olso on themselves?"

"Pretty much. Israel emerged from the 1991 Persian Gulf War in fairly solid shape. The Palestinians had discredited themselves by siding with Saddam Hussein. Israel finally had put the lid on the riots in the West Bank. And the PLO was in Tunis."

"If I were Rabin," Frank said, "I would have asked my cabinet: 'How do we consolidate our advantage? How do we keep the bastards on the run?' "

Gordon snorted. "They could use you over there. You're not Jewish, are you?"

"No, Italian. And more grateful than ever that my grandparents left Europe.

"If my grandparents hadn't left Poland," Gordon said, "they'd have been murdered with the rest of the family."

"And if the Allies had fought the Germans according to the Israeli rules of engagement," Frank said, "the war would have lasted two more years, and not one Jew would have been left in continental Europe." Frank took another bite of his food. "I had a friend, Harry Summers, retired infantry colonel, died last year. Wrote the best book on Vietnam. He said anybody who thinks violence doesn't settle anything should go to southwestern France and try to find someone who can recite the Albigensian Creed."

# CHAPTER TWENTY ONE

"Any more on Korea?" State Department spokesman Richard Boucher asked from the podium.

In his peripheral vision, Frank could see no hands going up. He didn't want to swivel around to look at the back of the briefing room. Consolidated Press's customary seat was in the front row across the aisle from the Associated Press's. Like the allocation of office space, the seating arrangement was an anachronism long overdue for correction.

"Middle East?" It was Gordon's voice.

"Go ahead."

"On the disorders in Ramallah and other places in the West Bank. Does it occur to the State Department that these riots tend to break out when the going gets tough in the negotiations between the Palestinians and the Israelis?"

"I wouldn't make that correlation," Boucher said.

You wouldn't? Frank thought. Why not?

"The point is to try to reach a peace agreement," Boucher continued, "and we pursue that end whether there's violence in the air or not."

Slippery, Frank thought. What if one side never wanted a deal? What if one side is violating both the spirit and the letter of the accords? Shouldn't the State Department take public cognizance of that fact? Why the Olympian detachment on the part of the U.S. government?

If Boucher can flip off a heavyweight like Morrie Gordon, Frank thought, what chance do I stand? But, hoping for the best, Frank raised his hand and was recognized.

"Last year Palestinian and Israeli negotiators agreed to reach a final accord by September 13," Frank began. "That's less than four months away. But in the seven years since the Oslo Accords were signed, the two sides haven't come close on the key points of dispute: Jerusalem, refugees, borders. The United States stands behind the Oslo Process, yet the State Department won't say anything about possible solutions – how those problems might be overcome."

"Right," Boucher said.

"How can outsiders take the peace process seriously when the most serious problems go unaddressed?"

"These are difficult negotiations that relate to the entire future of the two parties," Boucher said. "We don't think it helps the parties reach the necessary trade-offs by laying out options and having public debates on them. In the end, you will see the results if we get them. If we don't, it doesn't matter."

Frank looked down to jot a note and noticed two specks of tomato sauce on his shirt. He didn't have time to check what might be on his tie.

"But viewing it from the outside," Frank persisted, "can people be forgiven for concluding that these problems are in fact intractable?"

"I don't think it's in our interests to declare defeat and go home."

Frank didn't think it was in the interest of either Israel or the United States for Washington to set the Jewish state up for a fall, but he had pressed the subject as far as he could that day.

"Following up," Frank continued, "does the United States have a position on the fate of the mostly Christian South Lebanon Army in the face of an Israeli withdrawal?"

"I don't think that's the kind of detail we can get into at this point," Boucher said. "We support the idea of an Israeli withdrawal from south Lebanon consistent with U.N. resolutions. We think all parties should work with the United Nations."

"I want to follow on that," Gordon jumped in. "You're offering all sorts of tangible and intangible assistance to the parties. But these people who have helped to maintain the security zone for Israel inside Lebanon are being threatened with treason trials. Is there anything the U.S. government thinks ought to be done to protect them?"

"Morrie, I'm afraid at this point I'm not able to get into specific aspects of the Israeli withdrawal."

Mealy-mouthed motherfuckers! Useless diplomatic capons! Frank allowed his mind to wander for the rest of the briefing. If anything significant were to be said, which he doubted, he would pick it up later from the transcript.

Fritz Kraemer had been right. Frank vividly recalled the Pentagon geo-strategist's briefing to Washington Times reporters and editors 15 years earlier.

"Never trust a diplomat," the anti-Nazi German monarchist and mentor to Henry Kissinger had said. "By training and inclination, they are people who believe every dispute can be settled by negotiation and compromise – and that's simply not true. If two men want to marry the same woman, for example, no compromise is possible."

For Frank, sovereignty in the Jewish homeland was a bride not to be haggled over.

Although Frank had been covering the State Department for only a short time, he already was tiring of the assignment. Diplomatic speech was evasive by definition, concealing as much as it revealed. Frank was a forthright man who saw it as his duty to challenge unstated premises, strip away obfuscation, and reveal the stark facts to his readers.

But getting a forthright answer from a State Department official was like trying to trap smoke in a bottle. Those masters of misdirection could deflect any question with a handful of stock phrases:

"There's nothing new here."

"As we've said all along . . ."

"Our policy hasn't changed."

"I wouldn't speculate on that.

"I don't answer hypothetical questions."

"We think both sides should return to the negotiating table."

World War III could break out, and response would be: "There's nothing new here, and I wouldn't speculate on hypothetical questions. As we've said from the beginning, our policy hasn't changed, and we urge both sides to return to the negotiating table."

State Department officials seemed to think that foreign policy should be left to the professionals, away from the purview of pesky citizens. They saw themselves as a permanent cadre whose mission it was to guard against the excesses of Congress and the naïveté of presidents. After all, politicians came and went, while the Foreign Service provided institutional memory. Who knew better than they, who were in it for the long haul? Of course, much of what they "knew" was wrong.

For example, they were under the delusion that the truth was whispered to them over coffee cups and what was screamed from the balcony could be disregarded. In fact, the reverse was true.

Kraemer had been right about something else: Even with a firm grasp of the facts, it's possible to know everything and understand nothing. Frank, as a historian, was constantly amazed at the blindness of genteel Americans and Europeans to the rationality of those different from themselves. Members of this coterie, from whose ranks the decision-makers were drawn, seemed incapable of comprehending that the cost-benefit calculus natural to them and which they presumed to be universal was not widely shared by the rest of humanity. How many of these risk-averse bourgeois, for example, would die for honor – or kill for it? Yet the cutthroats who filled the post-Cold War power vacuums killed not only for honor and gain and revenge and prestige, but also for pleasure.

The daily briefings were a farce. If the State Department had any real news to break, it would call in a reporter from The New York Times or The Washington Post – one who never attended the briefings and seldom appeared in Foggy Bottom – and feed him an exclusive. Those from other news agencies, who toiled daily in the vineyards, would be furious to see their rivals in the halls. The regulars knew they would be scooped the next morning and they couldn't do a thing about it.

"Thank you." With those words, the spokesman's assistant signaled that the briefing was over.

Frank walked briskly from the room. He had an idea for a story, but he paused and looked over his shoulder for Gordon.

"This doesn't add up," Frank said. "It's going to be a mess."

"Wait till the riots come to Jerusalem," Gordon warned.

# CHAPTER TWENTY TWO

"Tobias Moore." The editor answered the phone in the British style by saying his name instead of hello.

"Hi, it's Frank. Here's what I'm working on -- "

"First let me tell you that Armand liked your story about the dissidents inside Vietnam."

"Was it worth the phone bills?"

"Armand said you're quiet for a reporter, but you remind him a little of Homer Bigart."

"Wow! That's unexpected. And wildly generous."

Consolidated Press Editor-in-Chief Armand de la Pendrioche was a French count who had escaped to England in 1940, joined the Royal Navy as a teenaged sailor, and was wounded on D-Day bringing troops ashore. In a distinguished globetrotting career, he had covered a multitude of wars and interviewed every leader worthy of the name. Trim and youthful at 74, he showed no signs of slowing down. Frank was awed by Armand's energy and output.

Armand had known Homer Bigart, a legendary war correspondent for the New York Herald Tribune and The New York Times, in Korea and during the Vietnam buildup. Bigart had been dead for years, and Frank knew him only by reputation. Frank assumed that any resemblance between Bigart and himself was in personality rather than *oeuvre*. Still, it was nice to hear.

"Thanks for passing along the complement."

*"De nada,"* Moore said. "Now, what have you got?"

"You know Ehud Barak has been making noises about a unilateral pullout from south Lebanon. My angle is: What will happen to Israel's mostly Christian allies in the South Lebanon Army?"

"Interesting. Will you have it today?"

"Depends on what I get."

"Let me know."

"Right. Bye."

Frank flipped through his Rolodex and dialed a number.

"Press office." It was a young woman's voice with an Israeli accent.

"David Wolf, please. Frank DiRaimo from Consolidated Press."

"Just a moment."

"And who's this?" he asked on impulse.

"Avishag."

"Avishag the Shunammite?"

He was rewarded with a deep, throaty laugh. "Yessss," she answered playfully.

"Well, Avishag, don't keep me waiting. Let me talk to your boss before I'm too old even for you to warm me up."

Another peel of delicious laughter brought an unaccustomed smile to Frank's face.

"Hold on, please."

"Frank! How are you?" The man's voice had a slight Australian accent. Frank's instincts told him Wolf's friendliness was genuine.

"Doing well," Frank said.

"What can I do for you?"

"What are you guys going to do about the SLA? You're not going to sell them out the way we sold out the South Vietnamese?"

"You waste no words. Are we on the record?"

"I need something I can use."

"The situation is complicated."

"David, I'm a newsman. What am I supposed to report? That the Israeli Embassy says life is complicated? What is the policy of your government?"

"As you know, Barak has been a skeptic on Lebanon for a long time."

"All the more reason to have a policy in place."

"The situation is fluid. All I can tell you at this point is that there's talk of settling some of the SLA families in Israel and some in third countries, perhaps in Europe. Some, presumably, will stay."

"They'd have to be crazy to stay."

"It's their home."

"And Frankfurt was your father's home. Look, David, you're abandoning these people to their enemies. What do you mean 'some' might be settled in Israel? You have an obligation to all of them. Israel's enemies watch to see how your country treats gentiles who throw in their lot with Jews. How do you think this looks?"

"With events unfolding so quickly, Frank, it's hard to give you a definitive readout."

"Unfolding?" Startled, Frank reached for his computer mouse.

"I thought that's why you called. The withdrawal is underway."

"I didn't know."

"It's been on the wire for about an hour."

"I was in the briefing. Hold on." Frank clicked on a story and scanned the lead paragraphs.

"This is bad, David. It's blood to a shark. And you're getting nothing in return. What happened to the idea that you wouldn't leave until the Lebanese army replaces Hezbollah on the border?"

"Off the record?"

"OK."

"I think the Syrians had something to say about that."

# CHAPTER TWENTY THREE

Cheers and ululations greeted Ahmed Asfour upon the released prisoner's return to his village in the Samarian Hills near Jenin. Asfour's wife showed the reserve propriety demanded, but his children welcomed him exuberantly.

⊨⊨ ⊨⊨

On the Lebanon border, jubilant Hezbollah fighters jeered sullen Israeli soldiers watching from only meters away. The jihadists blared the horns of trucks abandoned in the precipitous withdrawal. They shredded Israeli flags and hooted in derision as they tried on uniform pants left in the laundry.

# CHAPTER TWENTY FOUR

Frank was grateful to Janet for the ride. It was better than taking a cab, and it gave him a feeling of human connection before hurtling into the unknown. Amazing that his first trip with the secretary would be to Israel!

As Janet pulled up to the State Department's 23$^{rd}$ Street entrance, Frank saw other journalists loading their bags into the luggage compartment of the bus that would take them to Andrews Air Force Base, Maryland.

"There with minutes to spare," Janet said.

"That's great. Thanks."

"Excited?"

"A little. I've always wanted to visit Israel. Maybe if I like it, we can go together sometime."

"No thanks. I see enough Jews in Bethesda."

Frank was startled. It had been a long time since he'd heard anything like that.

"What's that supposed to mean?"

"Frank, please, don't over-react. You always –"

Their voices overlapped as they spoke simultaneously.

"Over-react? You say something outrageous, and I'm not supposed to -- "

" – over-react when I say something."

" – react?"

"It was a joke, OK?"

"Don't take up a career in comedy."

"You spoil everything."

Frank checked his watch. "Well, showtime."

Frank exited the front passenger door and opened the rear door. He pulled out his travel bag and a smaller laptop case and started toward the bus.

"Don't I get a kiss?"

Frank stopped and forced a smile. He leaned into the driver's side window and gave Janet a peck on the lips.

"Thanks again for the ride. Take care of yourself."

With another weak smile, Frank turned and headed for the bus. He greeted the other reporters, loaded his travel bag into the luggage compartment, and boarded with his laptop. It was a pretty June day, and the ride to Andrews was pleasant. From his window seat Frank enjoyed unfamiliar scenery.

Upon arrival, the reporters were told to line up abreast in front of the terminal with their luggage at their feet. An airman came by with a dog that sniffed each bag. Then the passengers were allowed to enter. During the long wait he caught up on the news and reflected that it was good to be getting out of Washington.

When it finally was time to board and luggage was being loaded onto the aircraft, agents of the Bureau of Diplomatic

Security stood with clipboards at the base of the stairway leading to the fuselage. Each passenger said his or her name and was checked off a list. Frank boarded with his laptop.

Inside, Frank took a seat next to Morris Gordon, who was engrossed in reading. Frank was amazed by the roominess of the seats, like first class on commercial flights. After they were airborne for a few hours, the steward served a huge meal. Against his better judgment, Frank ate most of it.

Frank felt a kinship with Gordon but was reluctant to do or say anything the older man might take as presumptuous. When Gordon put down his book, Frank ventured to speak.

"I don't get it, Morrie. Why is Barak so hot for a summit now, when Arafat still is making demands no Israeli government could accept? Oslo has led people to believe that Israel can end the conflict by making concessions. So if the summit doesn't pan out, the world will think it's because Israel hasn't made enough concessions. No matter how sweet the deal, Arafat can walk away, turn up the heat, and demand more later – with Israel's last offer as a starting point."

"Barak is a lone commando." Gordon said. "It's how he's always operated. He's his own defense minister, and he's cut his foreign minister out of the action. He knows that implementing the terms of a peace settlement will cost a bundle, and he's counting on Clinton to deliver Congress. Clinton's looking for a foreign policy legacy, but there'll be a new president in January. Barak would rather deal with the known than the unknown. Besides, Barak's afraid that Israelis are growing weak – tired of the endless struggle. He's desperate for a deal, and it shows."

"Meanwhile, Arafat has all the time in the world," observed Frank. "When he says he must have Jerusalem, he invokes a longstanding Muslim assertion. He even claims to be safeguarding Christian interests! Arafat thinks in millennia. Barak thinks in months."

"I used to believe Arafat was playing chess, and Barak was playing checkers," Gordon said. "Now I think Arafat is playing chess, and Barak is playing solitaire."

Before Frank could answer, a young female aide to Madeleine Albright appeared at the front of the cabin.

"Guys, the secretary is coming back to take your questions."

The reporters scrambled for their tape recorders and notebooks. Some stood in anticipation. Albright entered with a small entourage, and the reporters clustered around her holding out microphones. Albright looked tired but also self-satisfied, almost smug, as if her fatigue was a sign of virtue and testimony to her own importance. She seemed to expect appreciation for the efforts that had left her drained.

"Madam secretary," a voice called out, "are the two sides any closer to an agreement?"

"We should remember that neither side will get 100 percent of what it wants," Albright said. "We're going to assess whether a summit would be useful at this point or whether more work needs to be done."

"Would it be fair to say," asked another voice, "that the administration has staked a lot of its foreign policy credibility on the outcome?"

"President Clinton has a passion for peace," Albright replied. "The world ought to know that if working 20 hours a day is not enough for us to achieve Middle East peace, we will work 24 hours a day!"

Frank's face showed alarm.

"But that doesn't mean everything will happen quickly," Albright continued. "This is an important moment, and we have to keep working on the process. Out of frustration pearls are born, as every oyster knows."

"Last question," said a member of Albright's State Department retinue.

Gordon spoke up. "Could some thorny issues be postponed for resolution after a possible summit?"

"I wouldn't speculate on that," the secretary of state said.

"Thank you," the spokesman said to the reporters, signaling a conclusion.

"Thank you," the reporters chorused.

Albright and her group exited toward the front of the plane, and the journalists resumed their seats.

"Did you ever hear of a worse negotiating strategy?" Frank said to Gordon. "It's like you said. You never want to let it slip that you're so desperate for a deal you'd do almost anything to get it. Did you know my former boss, the late Beth Brenner?"

"I met her only a couple of times, but I read her columns."

"I remember her saying that her father, who sold antiques in Seattle, never made that mistake."

# CHAPTER TWENTY FIVE

Frank dozed fitfully on the plane but envied those, like Gordon, who could sleep for hours as if they were home in bed. He appreciated the spaciousness of the seat and reminded himself how much more comfortable it was than being cramped in coach on a long commercial flight. Still, he couldn't manage to slumber long. His dreams began while he still was awake. Surreal images in inexplicable sequences took shape behind his eyelids. What did that mean? Did it happen to everybody? Sometimes he would drop off for 15 minutes only to be jolted awake, his neck stiff, discovering that his front teeth had chewed a spot raw on the inside of his lower lip.

They landed at Ben Gurion Airport a few hours after dawn. Agents of the Bureau of Diplomatic Security jumped up, grabbed their gear from the overhead bins, and hurried off the aircraft. Wide awake, Frank took his first look at Israel through the window. With the other reporters, he descended to the runway, where a U.S. Embassy motorcade awaited Albright's arrival. The journalists and their luggage were loaded into white vans, which followed Albright's vehicle on the road to Jerusalem.

Frank's quiet enthusiasm was almost childlike as he took in the scenes through the window. His excitement grew as the motorcade left the heat, bustling traffic, and irrigated fields of the coastal plain and ascended to the relative coolness of the rocky and arid Judean hills. He saw what looked like antique armored cars that had been preserved as roadside museum pieces and wondered if they had been left there as reminders of the costly effort to relieve besieged Jerusalem during the 1948 Independence War.

Inside the city, Frank was charmed by Jerusalem's limestone buildings and the synthesis of old and new. From the van's window Frank noticed an attractive traffic policewoman, her dark hair pulled back beneath her cap.

Security personnel sealed the entrances of the Hilton's parking garage as those in Albright's motorcade disembarked and headed with their luggage to the elevator. Frank admired the bright, spacious lobby as he stood in line to check in.

In the privacy of his room, Frank started to relax. It was mid-afternoon, and he had a few hours to himself before the press conference that evening between Albright and Prime Minister Ehud Barak. He ran a wet washcloth over his face, changed into a suit, and left to explore Jerusalem.

Frank turned right out of the hotel entrance and walked toward the Old City, which lay golden in the sunlight. Jerusalem was magic, and Frank felt the spiritual pull that so many others before him had experienced. Truly Jerusalem was God's headquarters, the heart of the whole world.

Frank headed for the Jaffa Gate. As he passed over a pedestrian bridge, he was spotted by a handful of beggar boys, presumably Arab, who importuned him for money. Frank had no Israeli currency, so he took U.S. quarters from his pocket, gave one to each boy, and walked on. The boys looked at the coins in surprise and then chased Frank in indignation, waving their fists. Frank shrugged and continued on his way.

He must have had "tourist" written all over him. Inside the Ottoman walls, only moments after he passed through Jaffa Gate, an Arab appeared and politely asked Frank, in English, if he would like to peruse the merchandise in his cousin's shop. Frank declined. The Arab then offered to guide Frank on a tour of the Old City. Why not? They agreed on a price, which Frank paid in U.S. dollars.

Inside the Old City, Frank was transported to another world. He walked the narrow, winding streets as if in a dream. The markets, stalls, shops, and the dozens of religious sites enchanted him. The only disappointment was the Church of the Holy Sepulcher. He found the sections he visited to be gloomy and a little spooky. The décor was vulgar and overdone. Was this really the site of the crucifixion? Had Jesus really been entombed here? He returned to the hotel with the feeling that he had just scratched the surface of something immense.

That evening the auditorium at the prime minister's headquarters was packed with reporters from around the world, and seats in the front rows were reserved for those traveling with Albright.

At first Ehud Barak spoke through an interpreter, a woman whose English was halting and heavily accented, but before long the prime minister dismissed her and addressed the gathering directly in English. Morris Gordon winced and whispered to Frank that Barak shouldn't have done that. Frank admired Gordon's soft-heartedness, but he could see the prime minister's point. Barak's command of English was at least as good as the interpreter's, and his accent no worse. Why waste everybody's time going back and forth between languages and dragging the proceedings out to twice their required length? However, Frank did think the incident betrayed disarray in the prime minister's office – maybe even incompetence. Israel was full of people with total proficiency in both languages. Barak either should have decided in advance that his English was up to the occasion or arranged for the services of a real bilingual. Frank wondered what deficiency on the part of Barak or his staff had resulted in this poor woman being set up for public humiliation. Was it laziness? Indifference? Carelessness? Arrogance?

Frank studied the premier. Inescapably arrogant, he concluded. An organization always reflects its leader, and the cocky and dismissive Barak embodied the hauteur sometimes found in physically small men.

"A substantial negotiation will begin only if and when there will be a summit meeting," Barak said.

Frank asked himself why no "substantial negotiations" had taken place in seven years of "confidence building"? What the hell had they been doing all that time?

"And we will negotiate only an agreement that will strengthen Israel," Barak went on. "I will not sign on an agreement that will not represent the vital security national interests of the State of Israel."

Frank wondered if opinions differed as to what constituted such national interests. Did it mean selling out the settlers, as Barak just had sold out the South Lebanon Army?

"And I am confident that if there will be a summit, and if through a summit there will be an agreement, this agreement will be confirmed or approved by a landslide majority of the Israeli electorate – and, what is more important, by an absolute majority of the Israeli settlers in Judea, Samaria, and the Gaza Strip."

Was the prime minister talking about a referendum -- one in which Barak expected most of the settlers to vote to uproot themselves?

Albright took the podium. "Discussions will continue on all interim- as well as permanent-status issues," she said. "And I think the important point here is to keep working and dealing with what are clearly very complicated and difficult issues."

Blah, blah, blah. Frank had no confidence in Albright, and he'd earned that opinion honestly. In Yinglish, he knew "from" Albright. He and the secretary of state had a history.

Eleven years before, in 1989, when Frank was scuffling for a living after leaving The Washington Times, he tried to support himself by selling water filters. One of his Georgetown customers liked her filter so much that she referred him to her friend Madeleine. Frank called for an appointment and went to Albright's home on 34ᵗʰ Street with his brochures. Albright reviewed the models and decided she wanted the most expensive one – the whole house filter. Frank explained that this was the only model he didn't have in his inventory and the only filter he couldn't install himself. It required a licensed plumber.

He would have to put in a special order to the company, and he couldn't return it, so she had to be sure she wanted it. She said she was sure she wanted the whole house filter because she liked to take long baths.

In due course Frank dropped off the filter, and the house-keeper was ready with the check. Cut and print. Frank sent most of the money to Minnesota for the kids.

But then Albright called. She wanted him to pick up the filter and refund her money. The plumber had said the filter would cut water pressure in the old Georgetown house with its narrow pipes. Frank gently reminded her that this was a special order made at her request. He couldn't refund her money because the supplier wouldn't reimburse him. She was indignant but rang off.

The calls continued, progressively more insistent. Frank explained that the money was spent, that he was unemployed and sold filters to get by. He even went over to try to reason with her personally. "I'm just a housewife," the future foreign minister told him to his face. "You took advantage of me."

Frank was incredulous. You fucking bitch, he thought. Housewife? If Michael Dukakis had won the election, you'd be secretary of state right now. But he held his temper and said only temperate things.

As Albright's phone calls became harsher and more strident, she changed her mode of attack. She let it be known that she was an important person and intimated that she could make things tough for him. It was the Washington equivalent of Hollywood's "you'll never eat lunch in this town again."

Janet became worried. Frank had applied for a position in Beth Brenner's Editorial Department. He'd been out of work for a long time. Maybe the two Georgetown dowagers knew each other. Maybe they even had lunch! Frank couldn't take the chance. He scraped up the money for the refund, picked up the cumbersome and useless filter, and ate the loss.

Woman of the people. Scourge of the Serbs. And now she was going to bring peace to the Middle East.

＊＊＊

It was late when Frank finally filed his story, and he was hungry. He raced to the dining room of the luxury hotel a few minutes before closing and found it deserted.

"Is it too late for me to get something?" he asked the sweet-faced young waitress.

"No, you can order," she said, but she cast an uncertain glance toward the kitchen.

"Let's keep it quick and simple. How about if you bring me some hummus, some feta cheese, pita, and tabouli?"

"Oh, you want a dairy meal!"

Jewish dietary laws were the farthest thing from Frank's mind. It was just what he felt like eating and something that could be prepared in a flash. The food was served with olives, pickles, and a raw vegetable garnish. Frank ate with gusto and with the intent not to delay the waitress and the kitchen staff.

The waitress beamed. "That's the best meal I served all night!"

Frank felt warm inside. It seemed like the nicest thing anyone had said to him in a long time.

# CHAPTER TWENTY SIX

Ramallah. So near and yet so far. Headquarters of the arch-fiend Arafat and his Palestine Liberation Organization. Israel's "peace" partner. More like piece. Or pieces. Frank exited the hotel early for the trip to Ramallah with Albright's team and found several of his fellow reporters already depositing their computer bags into two white vans provided by the U.S. Embassy in Tel Aviv.

"Good morning," Frank said to Eleanor MacDougal. "Ready for Ramallah?"

"I'm pumped," Eleanor replied. She was a carnivorous journalist, far more competitive than Frank, but also generous with her knowledge. Because it was Frank's first trip to the Middle East, he had asked Eleanor for background information, which she readily supplied. She had an appointment to interview Foreign Minister David Levy – a Moroccan Jew -- in French, and she was reading Turgenev in Russian.

Movement to Frank's right drew his attention. There, under a set of arches at the hotel entrance, a handful of uniformed young Israelis stood in varying degrees of vigilance. Some were off duty, taking a cigarette break, but Frank could see that others were keeping a close eye on things. The sight of these boys and girls choked Frank up, and his eyes filled with tears. The emotion took him by surprise, as it had when the young man asked him if he would go to Vietnam again. The scene was all the more poignant for its simplicity. With enemies all around, these young people were standing guard, protecting their tribe. Something about this was so elemental, so primal, that it stirred Frank's soul. As with the young man at the university, he felt the presence of something precious that had been devalued, discarded, and finally redeemed. It was like discovering a unicorn on a lost island.

A cell phone rang. One of the soldiers took a few steps toward Frank and answered it. He spoke in Hebrew and then continued in near-native American English.

"I'm out in front of the hotel now. . . . See ya."

"Are you from the States?" Frank asked.

"Naw. I was born here. But I lived four years in New Jersey."

"What took you there?"

"Well, after my parents divorced – "

"Sorry. I didn't mean to – "

"It's OK. After my parents divorced, my Mom decided to go to grad school in the States. She has a sister there, married to an American guy. So we had family close by."

"Did you like it?"

"I was nice, but we always meant to come back."

Frank extended his hand.

"Frank Di Raimo," he said.

They shook hands.

"Gil Tamir. Are you a tourist?"

"Reporter. I'm here with Secretary Albright."

"Albright? Those settlers don't like her much. Did you hear the crowds demonstrating outside the hotel last night? 'Albright, go home! Albright, go home!' "

"I was out here and heard that. But then they chanted things in Hebrew I couldn't understand."

"Oh, it was something like: 'We know the Palestinians. We live with the Palestinians. They don't want peace!' "

"Are they right?"

"Could be."

Frank noticed the soldier's laundry bag.

"Do all Israeli soldiers carry their laundry around with them?"

"Oh, this isn't like the U.S. Army, where everything has to be starched and pressed. Israel is so small, lots of soldiers bring their laundry home for their mothers to do on weekends. I have a three-day pass, and my mother's coming to pick me up. There she is!"

A car pulled up to the hotel entrance driven by an attractive brunette who appeared to be in her forties. A stunning girl of about 17 jumped from the front passenger seat and got in the back, presumably to make room for her brother and his rifle.

"Hey, Mom," Gil said, "this is Frank. He's from -- "

"Well, originally from Cleveland. But I've lived in Washington for a long time."

"Welcome to my country."

"I love being here."

Was it Frank's imagination, or was there chemistry?

"We're having dinner tonight in Abu Ghosh. It's an Israeli Arab village not far from here. It's not fancy -- "

"I don't need fancy."

"They have hummus," Gil said, "not Hamas."

"Would you like to join us?" the woman asked.

"I'd love to," Frank said, "but I've got to get my story written -- "

" – He's a reporter," Gil informed his mother.

"There's a press conference at Arafat's headquarters in Ramallah." Frank thought fast. "Sure, I'll have it done."

"You're staying at the hotel?"

"Yes."

"We'll swing by about 7 o'clock. If you can't make it, leave word at the desk. Gil can run in and check."

"Great!"

Gil threw his laundry bag into the back and took the front passenger seat with his rifle.

"See you," the woman said.

"I don't even know your name."

"Dahlia. Dahlia Tamir."

She put the car in gear and drove off.

"Better hurry, Frank."

Eleanor's voice brought him back from his reverie. Frank turned to see his colleagues entering the vans. Frank picked up his computer bag and trotted to the nearest vehicle.

# CHAPTER TWENTY SEVEN

Frank took a seat behind the driver, who looked to be Israeli. The man in the front passenger seat turned and extended his hand.

"Hal Henderson, from the U.S. Embassy."

"Pleased to meet you. Frank DiRaimo, Consolidated Press."

As the motorcade passed through Jerusalem's northern suburbs, the other reporters laughed and talked, seemingly oblivious to their surroundings. Frank looked out the window at the arid, rocky hillsides. He watched intently as the vehicles cleared the last Israeli checkpoint, manned by soldiers in olive uniforms, and passed through intersections guarded by Palestinian Authority police in charcoal-and-aqua camouflage.

Frank's face showed concern as they entered Ramallah. Something wasn't right. It was a fairly large town, but Frank could see little activity in the streets. Only packs of boys roamed about, moving in synch -- like flocks of birds or schools of fish. A pack chased after the van for a short distance, then changed direction as if all its members were components of a single organism.

"Intifada kids!" Frank exclaimed in a spontaneous utterance.

"Yes," said the driver, "and *those*," he pointed to the PA police, "were intifada kids too."

Henderson turned and gave Frank a disapproving look. Frank felt an instant affinity for the driver and an aversion to Henderson.

He said nothing more for the rest of the trip, but he grew more concerned as he studied the vacant shop fronts and garage entrances. Instincts for danger honed in Vietnam were triggered. This place is going to blow, he thought.

The convoy entered the sun-baked grounds of the Muqata, Arafat's fortress.

Arafat and Albright, surrounded by security men, stood in front of microphones on a low terrace. A few feet below them, reporters and photographers from around the world were assembled. As always, Frank listened for a "lead," the most important element of the story that would be summarized in the first sentence. So far, he was fairly certain it would be that negotiations between Israeli and Palestinian leaders, including Arafat, would move to Washington and that Arafat would meet with President Clinton at the White House on June 14.

Not terribly exciting. The story would be procedural rather than conceptual, and Frank was a conceptual thinker often bored by the mechanics of daily journalism. To him, the illusion of "balance" often amounted to giving equal weight to the reasonable and the ridiculous. And how can journalists claim to be unbiased when the very decision of what's newsworthy is highly subjective? Frank's natural role was not to convey information, but rather to impart meaning to information. He was aware that humans had evolved as hunter-gatherers, and sometimes he asked himself how successful he would have been as a primordial hunter. Clearly, he wouldn't have been the best stalker or tracker, and he wouldn't have had much patience for creeping silently around the woods. But he would have been the guy who said: "Why are we hunting here? The caribou migration route is over *there*."

⊨⊰· ·⊱⊨

A European reporter addressed Arafat. "Mr. Chairman, at the beginning of Mr. Barak's term as prime minister, you praised him as your peace partner. I don't think I heard that today. Do you think Mr. Barak is the sort of partner you thought he was in the first place?"

"I am not prepared to answer that question," Arafat said, "because I believe this question tends to destroy the Palestinian-Israeli relationship. Therefore, I will not answer that question."

# CHAPTER TWENTY EIGHT

Frank checked his watch and read over his story. He made small corrections and read it again. Seeing nothing that needed to be changed, he clicked the tab that sent the story to the Consolidated Press newsroom in Washington, where the day shift editors would receive, review, and publish it.

He left the hotel with quick steps, looked around, and bounced on his toes with nervous energy. The day had been warm, but a refreshing breeze arrived with the evening. He still found it hard to believe that he finally was in Jerusalem! He scanned the passing traffic on King David Street for cars that looked like Dahlia's. King David Street! Here such a name wasn't symbolic or metaphorical or derivative. It was the real thing.

Twice his hopes were raised, once by a car turning into the entrance. A well-dressed couple Frank hadn't noticed behind him, speaking French, entered the vehicle. As he watched the car drive off, he was startled by the tap of a horn.

"You made it!" Dahlia said.

"Yes, shalom."

Gil stepped from the front passenger seat, offered it to Frank, and got in the back with his sister.

"Oh, thanks," Frank said.

Dahlia turned left at Agron and drove up the hill.

"What's that open area?" Frank asked.

"*Gan* – How do you say it in English?" Dahlia asked her children.

"Independence Park," said Gil.

Independence! Just so. Independence after 2,000 years. Frank wondered if any of his ancestors had besieged Jerusalem and destroyed the Second Temple in 70 AD, or had put down the Bar Kochba Rebellion 65 years later. But that was then. This is now.

They continued west, crossing King George Street.

"A windmill!" Frank said in surprise. "Are we in Holland?"

"The Greek church built that in the 1800s," Gil said. "I don't think it was used much. Now it's a shopping center."

They drove along a tree-lined road with an inviting residential district to the right. The car merged onto a major artery. On the left they passed green parkland, and Frank could see large modern buildings across the lawns. They went down a hill, under a bridge, and onto the main highway to Tel Aviv.

Dusk was descending upon the Judean Hills, giving them a purplish cast. Frank couldn't believe his luck – the company and the setting.

"How was Ramallah?" Dahlia asked.

"Scary. I haven't felt such cold fear since Vietnam. And I was only really scared there a few times."

"Were you a reporter?"

"No. Soldier. Engineer battalion."

"What was so scary about Ramallah?"

"I'll tell you at dinner. Where did you say we're going?"

"Abu Ghosh. It's the only Arab village in the Jerusalem area that stayed neutral in the Independence War, and the people are friendly to Jews. Most consider themselves loyal Israelis."

"Still, they've lost a lot of their land." The young woman's voice came from the back seat.

Frank, impressed, turned and gave the girl a look of respect. She resembled her mother but was even better looking. Frank tried to imagine Dahlia at the same age. No mistake. It wasn't just the years.

"Well, I know your brother's name, and your mother's -- "

"She's Nurit," Dahlia said before the girl could answer.

"So, Nurit. You say the Arabs of this town lost a lot of their land despite their loyalty? That's bad. Friendship should be rewarded."

Gil spoke up. "Sometimes I think Jews treat their enemies better than their friends."

"Gil!" Nurit exclaimed.

"It's true," Gil said sadly.

They pulled off the highway and entered Abu Ghosh. Frank loved its timeless, picturesque quality, like a pilgrim's postcard from the 19th century. And to think two days ago he had been on the streets of Washington.

Dahlia and her children looked out the car windows, spoke in animated Hebrew and gestured toward old stone buildings.

An Anglo-Saxon might have assumed they were arguing, but Frank guessed that Israelis, like Italians, held conversations that sounded like arguments to outsiders. As near as Frank could tell, the three simply were trying to find the desired restaurant, which stood among several others. After sounds of agreement, they rounded a corner and turned into a parking lot.

As they exited the car, an Arab man approached and greeted them in accented Hebrew. He escorted them into the restaurant, where Dahlia indicated a quiet corner table. The Arab host held Dahlia's chair, and Frank did the same for Nurit.

"It's good you're here with Albright," Dahlia said. "Maybe with all that's going on, soon we'll have peace."

"I don't think so."

"Why not?"

"Partly because of what I saw today in Ramallah. The Arabs are preparing for war. I can't explain it exactly, but I can feel it in my gut. And partly because the Oslo process never made sense."

"I think you're wrong."

A voice emerged from the constant chatter in Frank's head. "Wise up," it admonished. "You meet an attractive woman who's nice to you, and the first thing you do is pick a fight. Play it smart, for once. Go easy."

But he couldn't. He wasn't put on Earth to ingratiate or to flinch from reality as he understood it. And he wouldn't patronize Dahlia by being less than candid, as if she were some frail creature who couldn't handle an honest difference of opinion. It would be like treating her like a child. He wouldn't want anyone to treat *him* that way.

"Look," Frank said. "It's meaningless to agree to something in principle if you avoid looking at the hard stuff. Anybody can do that. In this case, the parties have avoided looking at possible deal-breakers since 1993. Now they're about to hit a wall. And when Oslo fails, Israel will get the blame."

"We've tried everything," Dahlia said. "We can't go on like this. Israel has to have this deal."

"You're still here, so you must be doing something right. Don't assume things can't get worse." Frank paused and gathered his thoughts. "Look at it this way: A man and a woman decide to get married sometime in the future. But the guy says: 'Honey, this business of my other girlfriends, and whether we'll have kids, and if you'll quit your job – let's discuss these things, oh, in about seven years.' In the meantime, he wants her house, the car, and power of attorney. That's Oslo."

A waiter arrived and set down an array of appetizers.

"Thank you," said Frank.

Gil dove into the food, while Nurit nibbled daintily.

"Take just one example," Frank went on." Israel should have made it clear from the beginning that the return of Arabs to Israel proper is out of the question. If the other side can't accept this, then there's no basis for negotiation. Never was."

"But the Arabs also have much to gain from peace," Dahlia said.

"The Shimon Peres model. 'The New Middle East.' I heard two of Albright's aides talking on the plane. I couldn't believe it! They said Peres is right: Peace will come to the Middle East the day every Palestinian child has a computer. That's like saying in 1938 that Nazism will end the day every German child has a slide rule. It's nuts! Peres is a patriot, and he's done a lot for Israel, but he's an old socialist who believes all humans are economic animals who'll do what's in their material self-interest. It's not true. In fact, it's impossible to make peace with people who want you dead -- or, at best, a degraded remnant. Any concession to those who seek your destruction is seen as weakness."

"You talk like a settler," Dahlia said. "Are you making aliyah and moving to the territories?"

"I'm not even Jewish." Frank leaned toward Dahlia and lowered his voice. "I understand the Arabs because they're like my Sicilian grandmother. She came from a shame culture, where revenge against perceived injury could be pursued for generations. She never would have been bought off with a computer. Arab rationality is not yours. They don't want what *you* think is best for their children. The Arabs figure it took 200 years to get rid of the Crusaders, and if it takes another 90 years to get rid of the Zionists, that's OK – regardless of what it costs their children."

"We can't exile the Palestinians," Dahlia said, "and we can't control them militarily. So what's your solution other than to make peace?"

"I don't have a solution, but I know it's not in Israel's power to make peace. Only the Arabs can end the conflict. I don't know when that day will come, but in the meantime it's Israel's job to be indestructible. Otherwise, you might as well get back on the boats."

The waiter returned to take their order.

"Is the shawarma good?" Frank asked Dahlia.

"Everything's good," the waiter said.

Frank looked to the others, reluctant to place his order first.

"You go ahead," Dahlia said.

"I'll have the lamb. And the vegetable soup."

Dahlia ordered a fattoush salad topped with marinated chicken. Gil and Nurit decided to share the mixed grill for two. For the table, Dahlia asked for a large bowl of Abu Ghosh's famous hummus.

"We'll take some home," she explained.

"I think Mom's right," Gil said after the waiter left. "Oslo is irreversible. I've served in the territories, and I can tell you: Israelis don't want to control the lives of millions of Palestinians."

"Israelis can plant the seeds of peace," Nurit added, "and peace-loving people have been doing so for seven years and more."

"It's easy for you to talk tough," Dahlia said to Frank. "You don't have to live here. More important, you don't have to send your kids to the Army. Peace is the only answer. A Palestinian state is inevitable, and it's in our interest to have some kind of partnership with it."

"Jews haven't always been pure in their treatment of Arabs," Nurit said to Frank.

"The more reason you've given them to hate you," Frank replied, "the more reason you have to fear them. I agree that measures in the territories must be justified on security grounds. Anything that humiliates or inconveniences the Palestinians for no good reason must be stopped. But if you guys want to show concern for Arabs, you should start with those who have a claim on Israel's loyalty. It's not just the Lebanese Christians. During the 26 years it ruled the territories, Israel developed a network of friendly and cooperative Palestinian Arabs. Do you know what happened to them?"

Nurit shook her head "no." Dahlia was silent. Gil, with a look of surprise, slowly nodded "yes."

Frank pressed on. "Under Oslo, Yitzhak Rabin imported the PLO from Tunis to bust heads for him in the territories. He figured that a gang of car thieves and shakedown artists wouldn't have to answer to the Israeli Supreme Court or all the bleeding hearts you have here. But the PLO didn't bust the heads of Hamas. Instead, it hunted down and murdered the Arabs friendly to Israel. Oslo was not only stupid; it was an act of stupefying disloyalty. Perfidious! It betrayed friends and betrayed weakness. You can't buy peace that way. No wonder Israel's enemies are preparing for war."

The table was silent.

"My stomach hurts." Nurit looking sick, returned a piece of food to her plate.

"My God!" said Frank, now profusely apologetic. "What a fool I am for going on like this. I should have known – "

"I'll be all right." Nurit paused to swallow. "Do you have a family?"

"A boy and a girl about the age of you and Gil. They're in college in Minnesota."

"That's far from Washington," Nurit said.

"Their mother lives there, and her health isn't good. Emphysema. We're divorced."

"Do you see your children much?" Nurit asked.

"Not enough."

"Why not?" Dahlia said. "You should. Bring them to Israel with you some day."

Frank smiled at the thought. "Maybe I will."

===+- +===

That night Frank had trouble sleeping. Thoughts about his personal life, the situation in Israel, and the internal dynamics of Consolidated Press flooded his brain, giving rise to discordant emotions. For a long while he lay in the dark with his eyes closed, covers pulled up, hoping sleep would come. His mind raced.

Dahlia really was an appealing woman, and she had lovely children. Any man would be proud to be their stepfather. He believed he'd made a mess of being a father to Don and Laura, and he felt the guilt of that failure keenly. Dahlia seemed to like him. Or was that wishful thinking? How much of an impediment was distance? After all, Israel was Dahlia's home. She was dug in. And although she and her family appeared to be secular, Dahlia still was Jewish. Would even a secular Israeli woman, one who dined happily on the un-kosher food of Abu Ghosh, consider a romantic partnership with an American gentile? Could he and Dahlia reconcile their political differences?

Trying to sleep was useless. He jumped out of bed and stumbled around in the dark looking for the light switch in the unfamiliar room, barking his shin on a chair. After much groping of walls and furniture, he found the switch and flipped on the light. For a few minutes he paced, then he hit the power button on the company's laptop. CP didn't expect another story from him until tomorrow. This one would be a bonus. He wrote a news analysis summarizing all the misgivings he had expressed to Dahlia and sent it on to Washington.

# CHAPTER TWENTY NINE

"Armand wasn't at all happy with your analysis," Tobias Moore told Frank in the Consolidated Press newsroom. "In fact, he would have spiked it if he'd seen it before it was published."

Frank was disappointed but not entirely surprised. Armand viewed the Middle East with European eyes. Frank tried not to appear overly defensive as he made his case.

"Tobias, everybody's missing the real story out of the Middle East. They're all looking to Camp David for results, but the summit is a distraction. It's no story -- unless you want to report that nothing happened there."

"Camp David is no story? It's the biggest foreign news story of the year."

"It's going nowhere. It will be a joke. The real story is the Arabs are preparing for war, and peace is an illusion."

Moore tilted his chin upward and looked at a distant point at which the wall met the ceiling. "Then we must report the illusion," he said, turned and ambled away.

Frank was dumbfounded. Did Tobias mean that Frank should expose the Oslo peace process as illusory, or did he mean that he should report the illusion as reality? Frank was pretty sure it was the latter, but he didn't run after Moore to demand a clarification. He was in enough trouble for one day.

"It was like a movie!"

How many times had Frank heard that hackneyed phrase? But Damascus in June of 2000, after the death of Syrian dictator Hafez Assad, was more like a movie than a movie. No screenwriter could have composed a scenario of such suspense. Central casting could not have chosen extras exuding such menace. And no set designer on any Hollywood back lot could have produced an atmosphere suggesting such danger. Every Syrian was on edge, and hard-eyed security men looked like they would open fire at the slightest provocation.

If I do what my boss wants me to do, Frank decided, I'll be killed.

Frank was scarcely back from Jerusalem before he was required to head back to the Levant. The day before he was to depart, Armand de la Pendrioche summoned Frank to his office, located several floors above the newsroom. In his long career, the French count had interviewed scores of world leaders, always looking elegant no matter how muddy, dusty, or squalid the setting. "You dress *up* for the Third World, not down," Frank had heard Armand say. No safari togs for diplomatic reporting.

Therefore, Frank wore his best suit when he reported to Armand's office. It was charcoal gray, tailored from a rich all-season Italian wool, set off with a crisp white shirt and a silk tie of a subtle silver hue. Frank had made the effort to look suitably ambassadorial, but his expensive English dress shoes hurt his feet, so he wore a pair of plump Danish mailman's moccasins he'd bought from a Massachusetts catalog outlet. He hoped Armand wouldn't notice.

Frank sat expectantly across from his boss's desk. Armand produced a business envelope and held it before him.

"Put this into the hands of Bashar Assad," Armand instructed. "Personally. No intermediaries. For his eyes only."

"Yes," Frank said. "I'll do my best."

Frank tried to keep an impassive demeanor. But what the fuck? Frank had heard Armand say that he – Armand -- had been the one to tell Anwar Sadat to go to Jerusalem and make peace with the Israelis. Frank had no idea how much truth was in this. Was Armand now trying to influence the new leader of Syria, an ophthalmologist who had lived in Britain? Armand's cousin was high up in French intelligence. Some things Frank didn't want to know. Even so, he had just agreed to be a courier.

There would be no beds or showers for three days for the reporters traveling to Damascus with Madeleine Albright, and travel tired Frank under the best of circumstances. True to form, Albright said on the plane that young Assad appeared to be a modernizer who would continue his late father's attempts to achieve peace with Israel. She also noted, as if it were significant, that Bashar Assad "likes computers."

Frank was disgusted. What could be more irrelevant? The real question was whether a 34-year-old eye doctor was tough enough to hold power in one of the Middle East's most brutal dictatorships. Bashar Assad had not been groomed to succeed his father. Rather, he became heir apparent only after his older brother had wiped out in his Mercedes. Frank suspected that if young Assad tried to make real peace with Israel, he would be assassinated like Anwar Sadat. But did Bashar want peace on terms any Israeli government would accept? Not likely, Frank thought.

A radio talk host had said that Albright looked like she should be changing sheets at the Red Roof Inn. Maybe that was harsh, but Frank would have preferred a chambermaid to Albright as foreign minister. After all, chambermaids must deal with reality and are not rewarded for flights of fancy. Frank recalled William F. Buckley's observation that he'd rather be governed by the first 2,000 people in the Boston phone book than the 2,000 academics who then made up the Harvard faculty.

At first Frank couldn't understand why Jesse Jackson was on the flight. Then he remembered that Jackson had gone to Syria in 1983 to urge the release of Robert Goodman, a black Navy flyer shot down over Lebanon. Frank always believed that the crafty Hafez Assad, after a show of reluctance, had been only too happy to place Goodman into the hands of a pro-Arab street agitator with no great love for Israel. This boosted Jackson's prestige in America and stuck a finger in the eye of the Reagan administration, which was perceived to be pro-Zionist. Frank recalled seeing the news video of Jackson emerging from the aircraft and raising Goodman's arm in triumph, like a boxing promoter with winning prizefighter.

Frank noticed that Goodman quickly had pulled his arm from Jackson's grasp. Frank liked this. He interpreted it to mean that the naval officer had not wanted to be Jackson's political prop.

Despite all this, Frank dutifully asked Jackson for his comments as Jackson passed Frank's aisle seat -- specifically, on the transition from Assad *père* to *fils*. Jackson said that Syria was at a crossroads, and now it was up to Bashar Assad to choose the right path. Frank took notes. Then Jackson said the same thing in one of his signature rhyming couplets. Jackson's expression was one of satisfaction and expectation, but Frank simply looked up and waited for Jackson to continue.

A look of annoyance flashed across Jackson's face. He repeated the couplet, punching Frank lightly on the shoulder as if in encouragement. Frank, immobile, continued to gaze up at Jackson. Jackson rhymed his lines again, this time striking Frank's deltoid with greater force. Frank picked up his pen.

"Jesse Jackson is punching me on the shoulder," he scribbled. "I'm writing this to make him stop."

"Thanks very much," Frank said, concluding the interview. Jackson, now satisfied, walked on.

Dennis Ross also was in the delegation. In the past month, Frank had seen firsthand the accuracy of Brett Lynn's characterization of the envoy. A briefing by Ross was like being hypnotized in a warm bath. The words flowed. The sentences had subjects and verbs. Heads nodded in stupor if not in agreement. The world lost its sharp edges. Boundaries blurred. A mellow fog enshrouded the senses. Waves lapped against the shore. Branches stirred in a gentle breeze. Sunrays filtered into leafy glades where does nuzzled dappled fawns. Bunnies nibbled tender shoots. Dazed listeners were lulled into acquiescence – but to what? After the briefing, puzzled reporters would look at each other, asking: "What did he say?"

A long, barren stretch lay between the Damascus airport and the city. Frank guessed that vegetation, and perhaps some dwellings, had been cleared to prevent ambush. Once in town, Frank could see the tension on every face. It looked like a coup, or even civil war, could break out at any minute. No sign of Bashar Assad. That was not surprising. Could Frank get close enough to Bashar at the casket to deliver Armand's letter? Frank was afraid that he would be shot if he tried. Still, Frank had not abandoned the mission. He was willing to take some risk. Maybe there was a way to do it without being killed.

It turned out to be impossible. The Syrians sequestered the reporters for two days in an empty restaurant. Frank didn't even get the chance to unpack his suit. Only Jim Dalgaard of the Associated Press was allowed out as a pool reporter. Dalgaard returned from the lying in state and dictated his observations to the other journalists. Frank was both relieved and disappointed. In a way, he had been looking forward to the challenge.

Back in Washington, Frank returned Armand's letter with mixed feelings. He would have liked to report a successful handoff, but Armand accepted his explanation with good grace. Frank never would know the contents of the letter.

# CHAPTER THIRTY

After never having been to the Middle East, Frank found himself returning to the region for the third time in the same month. He was in Ramallah again at the end of June, standing in the sun listening to Albright and Arafat.

The "chairman" welcomed the Secretary of State and thanked President Clinton for his efforts to advance the peace process and to ensure that the outcome would be just, lasting, and comprehensive.

Albright announced a surprise.

"I am very pleased to inform the chairman that the United States has established a $35 million scholarship program for students on the West Bank and Gaza to study in American universities."

A question was put to Albright in Arabic and translated for her benefit.

"Madame Secretary, Ehud Barak again reaffirmed the Israeli red lines on not giving back Jerusalem for any price and not going back to the 1967 borders. Do you think that the peace process offers any way for the Palestinians to bridge closer to the Israeli red lines?"

Albright replied that she hadn't read Barak's statement and therefore couldn't comment on it. But Arafat jumped in, his face flushed with anger. He threw the question back to the Arab reporter, reminding the world that Israel's stated "red lines" were meaningless, that Israel had relinquished land before after saying it wouldn't, and that it would do so again – this time to his Palestinian Authority.

"Why did Barak fully implement U.N. Security Council Resolution 425 in South Lebanon?" he asked indignantly. "And why did he implement Resolution 242 on the Egyptian track and on the Jordanian track? Even on the Syrian track there was an agreement related to the return of all the land and the removal of the settlements, as happened with the settlements in Sinai in 1982."

Morris Gordon spoke up. "Mr. Chairman, how do you proceed from here? The secretary said twice that it is now up to the Israelis and the Palestinians to do the heavy lifting. What happens next? And in your statement you thanked President Clinton for trying to save the peace process. Is it in critical shape? Is it critically ill?"

Arafat, who understood English, didn't wait for the translation.

"Perhaps you need to fully understand what I am saying," he replied in Arabic. "I do not need to repeat what I am saying, and maybe you will need some tutoring to become a success-ful journalist."

This was a mortal insult. Arafat's words were a breach of Arab etiquette, which honors indirect speech, and they vio-lated Arab laws of hospitality. Shockingly, Arafat had degrad-ed a guest in Arafat's own compound. Clearly, Arafat knew that Gordon was both Jewish and pro-Israel. (The combina-tion could not be assumed.) The "peace process" was Arafat's ploy, his indirect attack on the Zionist fortress and his way of winning favor in the West. Hadn't the committee in Norway already awarded him a Nobel Peace Prize? The wily terrorist was playing for time, and the "peace process" was essential to his long-term strategy of obliterating what he considered to be an upstart Crusader kingdom in the heart of the Arab world. Gordon's suggestion that the peace process might be critically ill struck at the core of this subterfuge. The veteran Associated Press correspondent, far from needing tutoring to become a successful journalist, was the only reporter present doing his job. Frank's respect for Gordon grew.

⟜⟜ ⟜⟜

Frank was in and out of Israel so quickly, he decided it made no sense to call Dahlia, who had given him her contact information. He wouldn't be able to break away from the dip-lomatic delegation long enough to visit. Maybe next time.

# CHAPTER THIRTY ONE

Journalists from around the world converged on a schoolhouse in Thurmont, Maryland, not far from the presidential retreat at Camp David. Anticipation was in the air. Would Yasser Arafat and Ehud Barak reach an agreement equal to that which Anwar Sadat of Egypt and Israeli Prime Minister Manachem Begin forged at the same location in 1978? Would the long conflict between Israel and its immediate enemies finally end?

Frank was pretty sure the conclave would go nowhere, as he had predicted to Tobias Moore. But, more than that, he *wanted* the summit to fail. Although Arafat was unlikely to accept any Israeli offer, he certainly would consider no offer that didn't entail Barak giving away the store. And Frank lived in dread of that.

Incrementally, Frank was abandoning a long-held belief. For decades he had assumed that retired generals brought to Israeli politics the experience and knowledge necessary to keep the state secure. For this reason, he had taken comfort in the accession of former chiefs of staff Yitzhak Rabin and Ehud Barak. But now he was coming to the belief that the military mindset actually was unsuited to confronting the challenges of political leadership in Israel.

Generals want to accomplish the mission. Finish the job! Get it over with! Do something! Do anything! If generals perceive that their mission is to "make peace," that mindset invites catastrophe. Rabin in his time fell victim to this syndrome in his disastrous embrace of the Oslo process. Now Barak showed signs of rashness, eager to finish the job started by his former chief seven years before.

And wasn't it Ariel Sharon, that fierce warrior, who as defense minister had demolished Jewish settlements in the Sinai? The "mission" then had been peace with Egypt. But before coming to Thurmont, Frank had gone to his files and reviewed a yellowing clipping. It was a New York Times interview from 1980 in which Sadat essentially admitted that he had suckered his Israeli counterpart, Prime Minister Begin. Frank had transcribed Sadat's words into his notebook. "Poor Menachem, he has his problems. After all . . . I got back the Sinai and the Alma oil fields, and what has Menachem got? A piece of paper."

A piece of paper indeed.

Frank had always thought the treaty that Jimmy Carter had famously brokered at Camp David was overrated – worshipped to the point of idolatry. It's true that Egypt had not attacked Israel during the 22 years since the Camp David agreement, but maybe that had nothing to do with the treaty that followed. Maybe Egypt was tired of losing wars.

Frank knew some people believed that Israel had brought the costly Yom Kippur War on itself. They held that if Israel had conceded to the Egyptians in 1971 what it gave away in 1978, then Sadat – in 1973 -- never would have unleashed his armies in concert with the Syrians. Many of these same people also believed Sadat's war aims were limited. He wasn't trying to destroy the Jewish State. He merely was jockeying for a better negotiating position, angling for future Israeli concessions, and striving to regain the national pride Egypt had lost in being defeated by Jews in 1948, 1956, and 1967. According to this school of thought, it was necessary for thousands of those stiff-necked Jews to die or be maimed in 1973. Didn't that court Jew Henry Kissinger advise President Nixon to "let the Israelis bleed" before providing them with desperately needed supplies? "Realists" such as Kissinger held that it was necessary for the Egyptians to think they had "won." This restored Egyptian pride sufficient for Sadat to travel to Jerusalem in 1977 and announce to the Knesset his desire to end the conflict. Therefore, Israel's pummeling in the Yom Kippur War was an essential precondition for amity and conciliation. It was Sadat's war for peace!

Frank considered this Orwellian Newspeak. What if Israeli forces had failed to rally in 1973? What if they had collapsed? Would Sadat would have turned his armies around, proclaiming: "That'll teach you Jews a lesson. Now we can make peace." No. He would have put an end to the Zionist experiment. In 1977 Sadat set out to get via diplomacy what he couldn't attain by force of arms. He was an Arab incrementalist, in it for the long haul. Then it was the Sinai Peninsula. Tomorrow it would be the Gaza Strip. At some distant point it would be the West Bank. And finally it would be Tel Aviv.

Unlike Kissinger, Frank had not wanted the Egyptians to have reason to believe they had "won" in 1973. He wanted them to know they had been defeated – decisively and in detail. When Egypt and Syria launched their Blitzkrieg that October, Frank was making revisions to his master's thesis and trying to mediate a dispute between two of his professors that already had delayed the degree by a year. He was planning to leave soon for Minnesota. Thus preoccupied, he at first wasn't unduly concerned by the news reports. Until then, Israel had been able to prevail handily against the odds.

Slowly – too slowly – he began to understand the seriousness of the situation. Reports flowed in of devastating Israeli losses of planes, armor, and personnel. The Arabs were advancing on two fronts. Frank was stunned. What to do? He didn't speak Hebrew, but maybe he could make himself useful as an ammo humper or a litter bearer. Perhaps he could get some guidance from the local chapter of Hillel, the Jewish student association.

On a beautiful autumn afternoon, he walked to the student union, wandered into the lobby and viewed the postings on the bulletin boards. Sure enough, Hillel was holding a vigil in support of Israel on the second floor. He climbed the stairs.

A group of women was engaged in a sedate folk dance. Deciding that the dancers were an unlikely resource, he looked to his right, where the sun streamed in through the window, and spotted a young man about his own age sitting alone on the edge of a radiator. He seemed to be agitated and a little disgusted. He had light brown curly hair and a three-day growth of reddish beard. This was no soft American hippie. Now we're getting somewhere, Frank thought.

"Are you Israeli?" Frank asked.

"Yes." His face and tone asked why his private thoughts were being disturbed.

"I wonder if you could point me in the right direction. I'm a Vietnam veteran and thought I might be able to -- "

"I'm a Six-Day War veteran," he said bitterly, "and even I can't get back to my unit!"

In this way Frank learned that commercial flights to Israel had been suspended.

Frank let it go at that. He rationalized that without knowledge of the language or Israeli procedures, he would have just been in the way – part of the problem, not part of the solution -- a danger to himself and others. In later years he came to realize that he could have done more. His U.S. Army Reserve ID card still was in his wallet. He could have made his way to an Air Force base and tried to catch a hop on one of the resupply shuttles. Maybe that would have been impossible, but he always felt a little guilty about not making the effort.

⇌ ⇌

In the end Frank had decided to take his entire Sadat file along with him to Camp David. He reviewed it as he sat in Consolidated Press's designated spot at one of the picnic tables that had been set up in rows for reporters at the school. Yes, there it was, in translation from the Arabic, 1975: "The effort of our generation is to return to the 1967 borders. Afterward, the next generation will carry the responsibility." And in 1980: "Despite the present differences with the Arab rulers who reject the Egyptian peace initiative with Israel, the fact remains that these differences among us are only tactical and not strategic -- temporary, not permanent." In other words, Sadat agreed with other Arab rulers about the necessity of destroying Israel but differed with them about the means of doing so and the timing.

So why did Manachem Begin fall for it? Frank had put that question to an Israeli professor living in the United States. "Begin didn't want to be remembered as a terrorist," the man had said. "He wanted his legacy to be one of peace."

Frank was repulsed by the very principle of "land for peace." It was a scrubbed-up way of saying: "If you stop killing us, we'll give you land." Pathetic. Who but a defeated people would acquiesce to such degradation? The currency in such a transaction was not land but Jewish blood. Why leave Europe for that? The Cossacks had nothing on Arafat. Rabin used to say: "You make peace with your enemies, not the Queen of Holland." But peace on whose terms? First you have to win; then you impose the terms. The Romans never would negotiate with an enemy still under arms.

Frank remembered the moment he became aware of the received wisdom about Jewish communities in the liberated territories. He hadn't been so shocked and appalled since, as a 3-year-old boy, his mother had confirmed that, yes, everybody dies. He could hardly believe that the world looked at these homesteads as nothing more than bargaining chips, sacrificial pawns in a larger chess game. What was worse, some of the Israeli politicians who sent the pioneers to settle the land had the same cynical view.

Toying with the lives of one's own people was not Frank's idea of leadership. He found it impossible to understand such callousness. Either plant settlements and keep them, or don't settle the land at all.

# CHAPTER THIRTY TWO

F rank sat at the long table between Morris Gordon and Eleanor MacDougal. Across from him, Brett Lynn worked a crossword puzzle.

"This is like a bad joke," Frank remarked. "How many reporters does it take to cover a news blackout?"

"I'm wondering if Barak does get a deal here whether he has the votes to get it through the Knesset," Gordon said.

"What do you think?" asked Eleanor.

"I believe he'll be able to do it," said Gordon.

"The briefing will begin in five minutes," the voice on the intercom announced. "The briefing will begin in five minutes."

The three got up, reached for their notebooks and tape recorders, and walked down the hall to the gym. The room quickly filled with more than 100 reporters and photographers who sat or stood before White House Spokesman Joe Lockhart.

"Good morning," Lockhart said. "I'll give you a little update of what's gone on since I saw you last, yesterday evening. I think we took you up through the two bilaterals that happened late in the afternoon. After that the president, the two leaders, and their delegations – somewhere around 40 people – had dinner together in the Laurel Cabin. The president, Prime Minister Barak, and Chairman Arafat sat at one table with about 15 or so of their aides. Secretary of State Albright hosted another table. National Security Adviser Berger hosted the third table, filling out the room. They dined on tenderloin of beef with sun-dried tomatoes, fillet of salmon with Thai curry sauce, roast baby Yukon potatoes, steamed green beans with almonds, a mixed garden salad, and assorted deserts."

Frank groaned. It was even worse than he had anticipated. Lunch menus! Table seatings. Worthless. Was he supposed to report that? He wanted to tell his readers what the principals had discussed, the sticking points, and how close the two sides were to an agreement. From being manhandled in the State Department press briefings, he had come to understand the U.S. government's position: any public discussion of key issues would undermine the negotiations. The State Department was explicit about it: No news was good news. So why was he here, camped out at the school and sleeping at a dreary roadside motel? If an agreement is reached, he could write his story from the press release. Hell, just publish the press release! In the meantime, he was running out of ways to say: "Again, nothing happened here today." And he *hoped* that nothing would happen.

He wished he had sources inside the negotiations who would leak developments to him. But he didn't – and none of his counterparts appeared to be scooping him on that score. Their stories were artful thumb-suckers padded with boiler-plate. Paradoxically, these called for uncommon skill. It was easier to report actual news than to pretend, day after day, that you have something to say when you don't.

But how many curtain-raisers can one write? Frank had gone into journalism as an expedient after leaving academia, but he wasn't naturally suited to the profession. His life's call-ing was not to be a conduit of information, but rather to pro-cess information. Even so, his news analysis from Jerusalem had been badly received. After one full day in Israel and the West Bank, he had concluded that Arafat was not serious about peace and in fact was preparing for war.

On his second trip to Jerusalem, Frank had overheard a pro-Arab, anti-Israel British reporter say that Clinton and Albright, fronting for Barak, were pressuring Arafat to ne-gotiate prematurely, before the necessary groundwork had been laid. But the two sides had seven years to lay the ground-work. Arafat knew there was no basis for an agreement. For example, he had not budged on the "right of return," nor would he. But no Israeli government, not even Ehud Barak's, would set in motion hundreds of thousands of Palestinians in Jordan, Lebanon, and Syria. Nor would it open Israel's doors to those millions worldwide who could claim descent from Arabs displaced from the British Mandate during the Independence War of 1947-48. Frank was sure that Arafat was only pretending to negotiate at Camp David so as not to appear intransigent. As usual, he was playing for time -- and he believed time was on the side of Israel's enemies. Arafat might not have wanted to come to Maryland in July of 2000, but he was eager to keep up the appearance, before a gullible world, of being Israel's "peace partner," a deception that gave international legitimacy to his gang of murderers. *That* was the real news.

Frank was beginning to understand why his instinctual aversion to Oslo had been justified. Inchoate intuition, like Marley's ghost, was assuming earthly form. The contours of a self-set trap were taking shape.

First, Oslo all but renounced Israel's claim to the West Bank and Gaza, where for many years Israel had sent pioneers to reclaim the ancestral lands. Judea and Samaria were the heart of the Biblical kingdom. Jesus had been born in Bethlehem *of Judea* – land of the Jews. But by embracing Oslo, Israel all but announced that it had stolen the territories it had redeemed in 1967. How, then, could Israel expect the world to applaud for returning part, but not all, of something it didn't own in the first place? And if Israel had no claim to the land, then "land for peace" was a contradiction in terms. Plundered territory couldn't be exchanged for a promised cessation of terror. Stolen property should be returned unconditionally. The premises of Oslo, far from winning favor for Israel from the nations of the world, were guaranteed to bring global opprobrium. To persist in the pursuit of a contradiction in terms was like charging off a cliff. Truly, it was a case of Jews outsmarting themselves.

From Frank's point of view, the world had made a fetish of the armistice lines that marked the end of Independence War in January of 1949. This cease-fire in place was no international border. But even if it were, almost every border in history was the result of a clash of arms. You conquer something in 1948, and you conquer something in 1967. Nineteen years. What's the big deal?

He was tired of people telling him that history had changed, that disputes no longer could be settled by force. Exactly when had history changed? With the establishment of the United Nations after World War II? But the original "United Nations" was the confederation of World War II Allies, a group of belligerents that certainly had settled things by force, had moved borders at will, and had generated millions of ethnic German refugees who were not blowing up cafes in their former hometowns. The U.N. organization that had succeeded the victorious World War II alliance was contemptible when not irrelevant, and it had kept the Palestinian "refugee" issue on life support for 53 years as a finger in the eye of Israel. "Nobody should be a refugee for something that happened in 1948," David Wolf, the Israeli press spokesman had observed. And Frank agreed. The United Nations, with the Western powers, in the lead, had given Israel's enemies reason to believe that they would win in the end.

Before coming to Camp David, Frank had phoned his sister for her take on things. He respected her opinion and considered her to be smarter than himself.

She offered this insight. "Suppose in 1865 the British and French hadn't accepted Appomattox. What if they had said: 'We understand that Federal forces have prevailed on the battlefield, but the success of the Union Army has not extinguished the legitimate national aspirations of the Southern people. Force settles nothing. It only perpetuates an endless cycle of violence. You can't kill an idea. We call upon Washington to withdraw from the 11 sovereign states of the Confederacy. End the Occupation now!'

"If that had happened," she said, "the Civil War never would have ended."

Frank knew that his confidence in his sister had not been misplaced.

⊨⊨ ⊨⊨

For long stretches, reporters lounged at the picnic tables in the improvised press center with little to do. Journalists kibitzed in several languages, mostly French, English, and Hebrew. Nir Golan, an Israeli reporter whom Frank knew slightly, sat across from a colleague. Unlike most of his counterparts, Nir leaned to the right politically. Nir said something in Hebrew, and the only word Frank understood was "Mitsubishi."

Nir noticed Frank's interest.

"I said none of us would be sitting here if it weren't for a 1992 Mitsubishi," Nir explained.

"What?"

"A car. It's how Rabin got the second phase of Oslo through the Knesset. The country didn't want it. Not the Jews, anyway. Rabin didn't have the votes. The thieves from Shas had left his coalition because their leader had been indicted as a crook, so Rabin had to depend on the support of the Arab parties. But even with the Arabs, he was two votes short.

"So Rabin bribed two members of a right-wing party. If they allied with the Labor government, they would be rewarded with cabinet positions and a car. So Oslo II was ratified 61 to 59."

"Why would anyone do that?" Frank asked.

"Those two guys? The word is that one of them traffics drugs, although so far there's no proof or I would have reported it. Rabin was an alcoholic. Who knows?"

# CHAPTER THIRTY THREE

F rank was pleased to discover a country buffet on the highway near the motel. He liked such places, which had something for everyone's taste. Take a little of this, and a little of that. No waiting. Modest tipping. You couldn't buy and prepare the same food for the price of a meal.

Although Frank ate heartily, one big plate was enough, and he seldom went back for seconds. But having nothing better to do on some evenings, he would linger in the restaurant after eating.

He couldn't believe the size of some of the patrons. Their tread was like distant thunder as they lumbered off for fourth helpings. Most wore shorts in the heat of July. Their calves were birch trunks, their thighs redwoods, and their hips sequoias. Brontosaurus! Thunder lizards! The words invaded his consciousness as he regarded his fellow diners. He had read somewhere that the brontosaurus never really existed. No matter. In his mind's eye, the behemoths still grazed in the misty ferns – a memory from his boys' book of dinosaurs.

But here and there in the vast eating hall were a few hard-eyed, wiry men with a 19th century backwoods look. They gave off a hint of danger, which made them interesting to Frank – solitary raptors in the sauropod herd. Frank surmised that if he were to have visited the area a century before, the ratio of raptors to thunder lizards would have been reversed.

He had brought a few books with him to the motel, but they failed to hold his interest. He looked around the dimly lit room and saw only a television. He hardly ever watched TV, and even less now with the Internet. But what the hell?

Eschewing the remote's confusing array of buttons, Frank put on his reading glasses, got on his knees, and strained to make out the writing on the control panel. He twisted the power knob to "on" and rotated the channel dial manually. He didn't see much. But what was this? Three young women singing. The brunette and one of the blondes were attractive. Were they sisters? The Dixie Chicks. Interesting name. And not bad musically.

Then, for reasons he couldn't explain, he was engulfed by feelings of loneliness, isolation, and frustration. He was tired of swimming against the tide, rolling boulders uphill, and getting his liver eaten by eagles. He was like a colonel without a regiment. He wanted allies, partners, a community, a tribe. He wanted to build – but build what and with whom? He yearned to associate with like-minded people, to be understood without having to explain himself. But even Dahlia Tamir, a serving IDF officer, couldn't see his point of view.

His kids in college, naturally enough, were busy with their own lives. Frank wondered whether Don and Laura would have had more in common with him if they had grown up in an intact family. Probably not, he decided. It used to be until you actually lost your marbles, the older you got, the smarter you became. No more. He couldn't program a VCR. He didn't recycle. He didn't even know how to use the wretched TV remote. His kids considered him out of touch and out of date, and they were right. Here it was the last decade of the 20th century, and his values were that of a bygone age.

Janet didn't like his new preoccupation with Israel. At first she had found it a bit eccentric and mildly droll, but now she was showing real irritation. She had picked up some funny ideas while living in Europe. She wasn't merely secular; she expressed a surprising antipathy to religion – Christianity no less than Judaism. Maybe he shouldn't have been surprised. He had dismissed her intolerance as a quirk when they started dating 15 years earlier. But now she was saying sophomoric things like, "Religion is the cause of all the wars and misery in the world."

Although Janet still could be sweet at times, she was drinking more now, which had a corrosive effect on her personality. For the first few years they were together, alcohol seemed to make her convivial. Now it made her mean. On a good night, she'd polish off a liter of wine. On a bad night, she'd kill one of those big liter-and-a-half bottles. "It's just wine!" she'd object when he suggested that she slow down. Right. As if wine didn't count. All this was taking its toll on what was left of their sex life.

She needs to find somebody who likes to drink, Frank thought, and I need to find somebody who likes to screw.

Frank enjoyed working at Consolidated Press much more than at The Washington Post, for he was appreciated there and allowed some autonomy. But although he had cordial relations with his colleagues, he had no really close friends at work. Frank identified with those who had agreed to accept a modicum of responsibility in the world, which meant that they were in charge of something. As long as they were not abusing their authority, he gave them a break. If other reporters weren't around, Frank pretended not to hear unguarded comments he knew could be damaging to the speaker. When transcribing quotes for publication, he cleaned up the grammar.

But Frank observed that most journalists enjoyed embarrassing people, especially "the powerful" – that is, people who had accepted responsibility -- as well as disfavored rural and ethnic Caucasians. They pounced on indiscreet remarks. They meticulously quoted infelicitous language. And they took smug delight in their assumed role of God's avenging angels.

When it came to Israel, the best of them seemed to think that Israelis didn't know what was in their own best interests. If only the Jews would coax Arafat into accepting their surrender, everything would be OK. Otherwise, Israelis would be out-bred by the Arabs, leaving two bad options: a Jewish minority ruling over disenfranchised Arabs, or abandoning the idea of Jewish sovereignty. The worst of the journalists were out-and-out anti-Semites who masked their hatred behind a pose of "even-handedness." Thankfully, these were few. Frank knew only one at Consolidated Press.

Nevertheless, woozy left-wing notions of Israel as the colonialist oppressor afflicted most of his colleagues, who romanticized Third-World insurrectionists as the aggrieved "Other" whose tender sensibilities had to be accorded the highest respect. Frank rankled at the suggestion that the hankerings of "The Other" should take precedence over the desires of one's own people.

On the television screen, the trio was finishing its song. He really liked the looks of the brunette. She was a younger version of Dahlia Tamir.

# CHAPTER THIRTY FOUR

Frank looked for silver linings during his sequestration in Thurmont. The school was architecturally uninteresting, but its classrooms had a cozy feel similar to that of his grammar school in Cleveland back in the 1950s. Contributing to this ambiance were small American flags pinned to the walls above the blackboards. But after a few days, the flags were gone. The State Department had taken them down so as not to offend the sensibilities of the Palestinians – or anyone else who might have taken offense.

Frank was flabbergasted. He knew the State Department had some good people, but he was steadily losing respect for it as an institution. He could understand banning the flags of the negotiating parties. But these were American classrooms in an American school. Why shouldn't the Stars and Stripes be displayed? Any foreigner who didn't like it could go jump in Chesapeake Bay.

The local congressman, Roscoe Bartlett, raised a flag on the school's staff, and Frank interviewed him on the lawn.

"This has incensed our people," Bartlett said, referring to his constituents, "and it has incensed me. How in the devil can these flags be considered detrimental to the prosecution of these negotiations? These people are coming to America. They shouldn't be surprised that American flags are here."

Bartlett said he had instructed an aide to raise the U.S. banner on the school's flagpole each day of the summit.

The next morning, as Frank was driving from the motel to the school, he was warmed by the sight of American flags displayed on almost every house and shop on Thurmont's main drag. Maybe there's hope, Frank thought. We might yet survive our feckless leadership.

Frank, leaving the lunchroom with a Styrofoam bowl of soup and a blueberry muffin, turned a corner and encountered a gaggle of reporters surrounding a handsome, dark-haired woman.

"We won't build another Iron Curtain across Jerusalem," she said with an Israeli accent. "This is something we will not accept."

The news-starved journalists were lapping it up. Finally, some grist for the mill!

But then, from the other side of cluster, a man approached with quick steps. Frank could see that it was Aaron David Miller, Dennis Ross's deputy, and Miller wasn't happy. Frank had lost some hearing in Vietnam, and it sometimes was difficult for him to make things out over background noise, so he didn't catch Miller's every word. But he got the gist. Miller was upbraiding the woman for using the media center to voice her opposition to Ehud Barak's peace efforts. He insisted that she leave the building at once.

But the reporters weren't going to let her go. Miller might speak for the U.S. government in the press center, but he had no authority in the parking lot.

"Who is she?" Frank asked Morris Gordon as the group exited the school.

"Limor Livnat," Gordon replied. "Opposition Likud Party. Former communications minister."

Frank, not wanting to miss any of this, decided not to chance returning for his notebook. He glanced back at the doorway and into Miller's baleful stare. Frank shuddered. What a creepy guy!

Outside, Livnat told reporters that Barak's policies could result in a "Berlin Wall" running through the center of Jerusalem, with the eastern sector under Palestinian control. "Jerusalem has never been a Palestinian capital," she said. "It has always been a Jewish capital." She also criticized proposals being aired by Barak to cede the Jordan Valley, long regarded as a vital military buffer against an attack from the east. Frank was impressed.

"Miller is a limp dick," Frank said to Gordon, who grunted noncommittally. But Gordon reminded Frank that two days earlier the State Department had expelled a Palestinian under similar circumstances. This was news to Frank. He must have been in the bathroom, or the cafeteria, or walking around the grounds. Regardless, this information didn't change Frank's opinion of Miller. Limor Livnat was his kind of Jew.

Opposing Israeli delegations took station on the grass across from the school. Visitors affiliated with Barak's ruling Labor Party, joined by American Jewish allies from the eastern seaboard, displayed their support for the policies of the prime minister. Israelis from the nationalist camp had made the trip because they feared the results of those policies. Frank spoke with both factions.

He established his credentials with Barak's supporters by telling them, truthfully, that he had been a member of Habonim – the Labor Zionist youth group – when he was in high school.

"I was the only Gentile," he said.

That loosened them up. They shook their heads in smiling wonder.

They were good people, even if Frank thought them naïve and misguided. Most of the men were combat veterans, some of multiple wars. One ex-paratrooper quoted a former commander as saying: "We trust Ehud." Frank kept his opinions to himself, but he had come to the belief that Barak's distinguished military record made him more likely to damage Israel's security, not less. The clear precedent was Yitzhak Rabin.

Frank was reminded of Rabin as he walked through the nationalist encampment. The right-wingers had erected panel after panel of photographs of Israelis killed and wounded since Rabin signed the Oslo Accords in 1993 -- hundreds of victims of all ages. Photos of the deceased were taken in life, but the bloodied faces of the wounded haunted Frank. Their eyes said: "We're still here. You didn't kill me *that* time."

Rabin had written off the first cohort of these terror victims as "sacrifices for peace." And for this we need a retired general? Frank asked himself. Maybe Rabin was drunker than usual when he said that. And Rabin had called Israeli conservatives "cowards of peace." Those he had so slandered now were documenting, in the most graphic fashion, the human cost of his folly.

The nationalists asked Frank if he wanted to speak with a "real settler." The boy, about 14, lived in the Judean hills but commuted by bus to his school in Jerusalem. What impressed Frank most was the boy's serenity. In his place, Frank would have been defiant and truculent. But the youth had the peace that comes with submission to a Higher Power.

"It's our land," the boy said softly. "God gave it to us."

Moved by the boy's innocence, Frank once again choked back tears. I guess that's the difference between faith and politics, he thought.

# CHAPTER THIRTY FIVE

The phone rang in the motel room, and Frank put down his book.

"Well, hello, stranger." It was Janet's voice. Her moods were unpredictable, but he was thankful that she seemed to be in a friendly frame of mind.

"Hi! I'm glad you called. It seems like I've been here a million years." Frank was grateful for the human contact.

Despite their differences, he considered her a friend. In fact, she was his only real friend who wasn't hundreds or thousands of miles away. He didn't seem to have had trouble making friends until he came to Washington in 1984. He and Janet had been together for 15 of those 16 years, and his entire social network consisted of people she knew. Now that he and Janet were living apart, he hardly saw them.

Maybe the Washington environment was unique, at least among the former valedictorians, class presidents, student council titans, and yearbook editors who flocked to the nation's capital every year. Area natives, both black and white, were more easy-going than these overachievers, who seemed to see others as potential competitors rather than as potential allies.

But maybe it was him. Perhaps he hadn't made the effort. Maybe he had become inflexible, indifferent, self-isolating, and unsocial. Who could say? Still, Harry Truman had known what he was talking about: "If you want a friend in Washington, buy a dog."

Janet had given him the station wagon he was driving. The transmission had failed, and she had spent a lot of money and time in multiple attempts to get it fixed. Finally, she bought a new car and was ready to junk the old one, but Frank asked if he could have it and found a shop that was able to do the repair. He had gone several years without a car, which was not burdensome in the District of Columbia, for he usually walked the two miles to work and took the bus back. But enterprise reporting required him to have his own transportation. Would Janet have been able to take a tax deduction for donating a junked car to charity? Frank wasn't sure. If so, she had passed it up for his benefit.

"Will this thing ever end?" Janet asked.

"I thought I was getting sprung tomorrow, but Clinton's put off going to Okinawa for a day. Maybe Thursday. Hope Barak doesn't make any rash offers."

If Janet had any reaction to his last statement, she didn't express it.

"Miss me?"

"Sure. Can't wait to see you."

"Oh, Laura called. She didn't get an answer at your place. No message. Guess she just wanted to talk to her Dad."

"I'll give her my cell phone number."

The phone was the property of Consolidated Press. His boss had insisted that he carry it, and Frank had resisted. He didn't like implements hanging off his person. An electronic device on his belt made him feel like a convict on a work-release program. And now that he was at the beck and call of anyone at the office, there was no such thing as being off duty anymore. But slowly, he was coming around. He had to admit that if his daughter wanted to reach him when he was on assignment, a mobile phone was handy.

"Well, maybe you'll be home for the weekend."

"Hope so."

"So long, sweetie."

"Good night."

# CHAPTER THIRTY SIX

The hour was late, and only about a third of the reporters occupied their places at the press center. Frank sat before his laptop reading a newspaper when he saw Eleanor MacDougal approaching in a rush.

She spoke in hushed excitement: "There's going to be an announcement at 11:00 p.m.!"

Five minutes later, Frank was among a relatively small number of reporters who gathered to hear spokesman P.J. Crowley. Whatever Crowley has to say, I'll get the jump on most of the others, Frank thought with some relief. For an academic, he was a lightning-fast writer. For a newsman, he was slow.

"The summit has come to a conclusion without reaching agreement," Crowley announced.

Frank was elated. The danger had passed! His prediction had been proved correct. He was vindicated. Now he could check out of the motel and drive back to Washington. But first he'd have to file a brief report. Apparently, the talks had broken down over the issue of Jerusalem.

Frank packed up his computer and his papers and went down the corridor to the briefing room for one last look. The atmosphere was like the circus leaving town.

People moved quickly in the halls. Frank spotted Nir Golan.

"Nir! What do you think?" Frank resisted the temptation to say that Israel had narrowly avoided a disaster.

"Did you know that Barak is issuing a statement at the Hampton Inn in Frederick at midnight?"

"I didn't! Thanks for the tip."

Frederick was on the way back to Washington. Reporting Barak's statements would be a perfect way to re-top his story and would give him a jump on the competition. It would be a feather in his cap. Consolidated Press management would be pleased. Once again the wire service would be leading the pack, just like in the old days.

But he had to move fast. He packed up his things and trotted to the parking lot, where he noticed that ground fog had gathered. He drove through Thurmont as quickly as safety permitted, reached the highway, and roared to the motel. In the bathroom, he snatched up his razor, toothbrush, and comb and tossed them into his shaving kit. He took satisfaction in remembering the little shampoo bottle behind the shower curtain. Then he tossed socks, underwear, shirts and slacks into his bag and took a last look around. That was everything.

He was lucky to catch the night clerk still in the office. Frank placed his room key on the counter with quiet deliberation and controlled his impatience as the clerk languidly prepared the receipt.

Frank knew a normal person would have had no trouble following the clerk's directions to the hotel, but he was easily befuddled about such things. He grasped the general idea. Close enough. He hit the highway.

Frank checked his watch and realized that he had little chance of arriving before midnight. But he also knew that Israelis seldom start anything on time and that Barak probably would make his opening remarks in Hebrew and take the first questions from the Israeli press. With any luck, he would arrive just when Barak started speaking English.

The fog patches thickened as he neared the stretch of highway where the clerk had told him to expect the hotel. He didn't know the landmarks, so he braked, craned his neck and squinted trying to make out signs. He checked the rearview mirror for overtaking headlights, but luckily the highway was sparsely traveled at midnight. Clusters of roadside lights raised false hopes. Where was the damned hotel?

Then, through a break in the fog, he saw it on his left as he whizzed past at 60 miles per hour. He needed to turn around, but where? Visibility was terrible. He would have to chance it. He slowed to 45, peered into the fog for approaching traffic, and accelerated into a U turn. Thank God! He'd made it.

The entrance was hard to see, so Frank considered himself lucky to discover that he was driving through the egress marked "Exit." At least he hadn't overshot the building again. He pulled to the right to allow an exiting car to pass, thankful that no one had yet blared a horn. This tended to rattle him, even though he knew it shouldn't. The parking lot was packed, and he had to drive around for several minutes until he found a space.

He'd arrived. He breathed easier as he approached the hotel entrance. He felt hopeful, competent, and effective. Was that a twinge of happiness? It had been so long, he wasn't sure.

But something was wrong. People and camera crews were streaming out of the building, not in. Had he missed the whole thing? A look of faint disgust on a cameraman's face suggested otherwise. Frank thought it unlikely that the man was reacting to what Barak might have said. Whatever that was, the cameraman had heard worse. Maybe the word about the press conference was simply incorrect. Perhaps all these people had been sent on a wild goose chase.

But that couldn't be the case. There, headed out of the hotel, was David Wolf. Surely, the Israeli Embassy press attaché wouldn't have been misled about where his prime minister was to speak. Frank threaded his way through the onrushing bodies.

"David! What's happening?"

"The summit is back on."

"Back on?"

"Back on."

"Holy shit!"

Frank knew Wolf well enough to see that the spokesman considered this to be a messed up situation, but as a foreign ministry diplomat he would never say so.

"Clinton is speaking at the school in a few minutes," Wolf said. Then he was gone.

Frank was numb. He entered the lobby as if in a trance, carefully placing one foot in front of the other. People eddied around him. Again, he was in the way. He lurched toward a vacant spot against a wall. On a TV monitor, a weatherman droned a forecast. The latest news from Camp David hadn't broken, but it would soon, and it would break without Frank. How to recover from this? First he had to call John Schneider, the night guy on the desk. Twice he tried the cell phone, but reception was poor and the calls dropped. Should he throw himself at the mercy of the staff and beg to make a long-distance call on a hotel phone? Or lie and say it's a local call? A real newsman wouldn't hesitate, Frank thought, but he didn't want to go that route. Suddenly, he remembered that he had two pre-paid long-distance phone cards in his briefcase that he had bought for just such emergencies. With a coin, he scraped the strip off one of them, exposing the account number.

The era of the enclosed booth had past, but Frank found an exposed pay phone down the hall. He placed his briefcase between his ankles and picked up the receiver. It took several minutes and almost all his change to figure out the sequence of when to deposit money for a dial tone and when to input the card's numbers.

"Consolidated Press, John Schneider."

"John, Frank DiRaimo."

"Yes, Frank."

"I'm in kind of a mess, and I hope you can help me."

"What is it?"

"I'm at a hotel in Frederick. They told me the summit was over, and I learned that Barak would be speaking here at the hotel. I figured I'd catch him on the way back to Washington. So I get here, and everyone is leaving, and I learn that – sorry, we changed our minds – the summit is back on."

"Wow!"

"Clinton is speaking at the press center in Thurmont. He's probably already started. For ten days, the son-of-a-bitch doesn't go near the school, and an hour after his representative announces the end of the summit, he shows up. Could you please cover Clinton off the television and re-lead my story with his comments?"

"No problem. Will do."

"Thanks, John. I owe you."

# CHAPTER THIRTY SEVEN

The atmosphere in Tom Sheridan's office was tense as Frank sat across the desk of the unsmiling executive editor. To one side, grim, sat Frank's immediate boss, International Editor Tobias Moore.

"You were caught out of position, Frank," Sheridan said. "It's a mark against you."

"They said the summit was over. Was I supposed to argue with them?"

"You were negative about Camp David from the start," Moore snapped. "That's why you ran out of there at the first excuse."

"We're taking you off the story, Frank," said Sheridan. "You've become too close to it. We're sending Margaret. You can watch the Pentagon till she returns."

Frank sensed an opening.

"Listen, the State Department beat has been wearing me down. Whatever you ask them, on any subject, they say: 'There's nothing new here. Our position all along has been that both sides should return to the negotiating table.' "

"Develop better sources!" Moore growled.

"I know, I know," Frank said, "but diplomats would rather withhold information than reveal it. That's what being 'diplomatic' means. How about my request to write features and some commentary?"

"We'll see," said Sheridan.

Frank was unsurprised when a wave of Arab terror broke over Israel two months later. At first he was more resigned than angry. He had done his best, and his conscience was clear. Besides, no one knew how long the violence would last. Perhaps it would be suppressed quickly.

But as the attacks grew more numerous, deadly, and brazen through 2001, his feelings hardened. Sure enough, low-intensity war was being waged against the Jews of the Middle East. Although he had predicted this, he was stunned by something he hadn't foreseen. The greater the number of Jews killed and maimed in Israel, the more unpopular Jews became outside Israel – even in the United States! Frank was shocked by a resurgence of anti-Semitism of the sort he had not seen or heard in 40 years.

He was grateful that he no longer was assigned to the State Department and obligated to transmit its equivocal platitudes.

# PART FOUR

# CHAPTER THIRTY EIGHT

Hadera, Israel
January 17, 2002

One would hardly know the joyous celebration was drawing to a close. Happy sounds of Russian, Hebrew, Yiddish, and English still echoed through the banquet hall. Older people paused for breath between dances, wiping their foreheads and admiring the boundless energy of the young guests gathered to honor the bat mitzvah of 12-year-old Nina Kardashova. In a change of pace, the band's Roni Ellis crooned a slow tune, with the back-up singers joining him in soft harmony. Roni, the son of African-Americans from Chicago, was Israeli born.

Heads turned toward a commotion at the entrance. A young man with an M-16 assault rifle, shouting in Arabic! He leveled his weapon and fired repeatedly, shooting as many people as he could.

What ensued can be described only in a catalogue of shattered bones and shredded organs. Those killed outright suffered least. Nina's grandfather was among them, as was Roni Ellis, who shielded a woman with his body and died.

Remarkably, as the terrorist paused to change magazines, the guests rallied. A truck driver threw a chair, hitting the gunman in the face, distracting him long enough for another guest to clip him with a beer bottle. With the fury of a lioness, Nina's mother grabbed the killer by the hair and slammed his head against the floor. Nina's father jumped on the attacker, beating him and revealing an explosive belt and grenades.

"Grab his hands!" someone shouted in Russian.

Frantically, the guests mobbed the murderer, restrained his arms, and dragged him outside, where a Jewish police commander and an Arab police volunteer shot the terrorist in the head.

Washington, DC
January 18, 2002

"The Al Aqsa Martyrs' Brigade – the military wing of Yasser Arafat's Fatah movement -- claimed responsibility for the attack, which took the lives of six and left at least 33 wounded at the coming-of-age party of a Jewish girl," the TV announcer intoned.

"This has got to be the only war in history," Frank observed, "where the civilians of one side are off-limits, and the civilians of the other side *are* the target."

"It's horrible," Janet said.

"Israel is paying for betraying its Lebanese allies," Frank said. "Enemies always see this as weakness and go in for the kill. And just as Israel is paying for its bad faith, so the United States will pay if it betrays Israel."

"But didn't Osama bin Laden say the Palestinian cause was one of the reasons why he attacked America?"

"It's always hard to tell what other people's real motives are," Frank answered. "Al-Qaida is at war with the infidel West, and the United States is the strongest Western nation. Bin Laden must have figured that if terrorism caused Israel to make unprecedented concessions, it also would make us lose our nerve."

Frank paused.

"I've got to go back," he said.

"To Israel?"

"Yeah."

"Why?"

"I'm not sure. It's like Vietnam. After I'd been home for a while, I found myself wanting to go back. I never understood that either."

# CHAPTER THIRTY NINE

Frank didn't have the same privacy in the Consolidated Press newsroom that he had enjoyed in CP's derelict office at the State Department. As he waited for his call to be put through, he swiveled his chair away from other occupied desks and faced into empty space.

"Hey, David," he said conspiratorially. "Listen. I need to keep my voice down. With all that's going on in Israel, I have to go back. But the company is covering the violence with stringers and won't underwrite a trip. Any suggestions?"

"How about travel reporting?" David Wolf offered.

"Travel reporting?"

"Hosted by our Ministry of Tourism. I think we can do this."

A week later, after the ministry had approved the trip, Frank approached International Editor Tobias Moore.

"How would you like some overseas bylines at no cost to the company other than my modest salary?" Frank asked.

"Who's footing the bill, and what's their agenda?"

"The Israeli Ministry of Tourism. The agenda, I guess, is to show that it's still fun to visit the Holy Land even when the Arabs are trying to blow the place up."

"Hmmm," Moore pondered. "I'll have to take it up with Tom. The source of the funding would have to be made clear in each story. If you do go, you must stick to travel writing. No politics."

"Right."

"Are they flying you first class, or are they putting you in the back with all the Yids?"

Frank's surprised expression was his only response.

⇥⊹⊹⇤

On his last day in the office, Frank rose to go to lunch as Jeff Hirsh, his neighbor in the next cubicle, returned from an assignment. Frank's curiosity (Janet would have said "nosiness") got the better of his discretion.

"Jeff, have you ever been to Israel?"

"No," said Jeff, dropping his notebook on the desk with a plop.

"I'm leaving tomorrow to do some travel writing there. It's a great place. Edgy. Intense vibes. Rich history. Pretty women. Food's not bad, although some like to complain about it."

"Never had the urge."

Frank knew it would have been polite to drop the matter then and there. Hirsh owed him no explanations. Clearly, he was uncomfortable talking about Israel and didn't want any more questions. But Frank was hungry for data. He wanted to understand. He needed to see where this would go.

"But you vacation in France and Italy," Frank ventured.

"Why are you asking me this?" Hirsh snapped. "Because I'm Jewish? You've got a lot of nerve! Don't tell me how to be Jewish. Let me tell *you* something. *As a Jew*, I have no use for an aggressive, reactionary, militarized, ethno-religious state. As a Jew! Get it? But just as I hate those things about Israel, I know you like the place for the same reasons."

From his seat near the galley, Frank looked up at the black-clad, bearded Orthodox men bobbing and swaying in prayer. A pretty Yemenite stewardess approached and said something to them in Hebrew, which they ignored. Then, in English, she asked them to return to their seats and buckle up for the landing. They shied away from the flight attendant as if her touch would contaminate. Grudgingly, they took their seats. As the wheels touched down, all the passengers broke into applause.

Frank stood in the aisle awaiting debarkation, and a surge of excitement overcame his flight fatigue. He deplaned and walked eagerly though the terminal, following the other passengers toward customs and immigration, glad to be stretching his legs. Frank was happier than he had been in a long time. He was where he belonged.

"Mr. DiRaimo?"

It was a sweet-faced girl of about 20 with wavy, light-brown hair and a faint bridge of freckles across her nose.

"Yes."

"Orna Arditi, from the Tourism Ministry."

"How did you know it was me?"

The girl smiled but didn't answer.

"Come with me, please."

Orna whisked Frank though customs and immigration. He retrieved his checked baggage and followed her out of the terminal. She led him to two men standing by a car parked in the loading zone.

"This is Arnie Mehlman," said Orna. "He'll be your guide for a week."

Arnie offered his hand.

"Welcome to Israel," he said.

"Thanks," Frank replied as they shook hands. "It's good to be back."

"And this is Uri Gabay," Orna said. "A ministry driver."

"Shalom," Frank said, offering his hand.

"Shalom," said Uri, smiling.

Frank thanked Orna as Uri loaded Frank's bags into the trunk. Arnie insisted that Frank sit in the front, next to Uri.

"You need to see," he said, getting into the back seat.

The three men waved farewell to Orna, and Uri rolled off for Tel Aviv. Night was falling as they entered the metropolis.

"You from the States?" Frank asked Arnie. Uri had the look of a native-born Israeli whose parents had come from the Middle East or North Africa.

"No," Arnie said. "Montreal. My family made aliyah in 1978."

Frank regarded the bustling city outside the window.

"Israel seems scary on television, but it sure doesn't seem scary up close," he observed.

"You know," Arnie said, "when people are afraid to come here and tourism tanks, it doesn't just hurt Jews. It puts the whole service industry out of work – taxis, hotels, restaurants – and many of the service sector workers are Arabs."

⊷⊶

At a safe house in the hills of Samaria near Jenin, Ahmed Asfour sat across a folding coffee table from a young man who looked both sorrowful and angry.

"Your brother's blood will be avenged," Asfour said in Arabic. "The Jews are on the run, and the end of our people's suffering is in sight. Hezbollah has chased the Israeli Army out of Lebanon, and we will follow their example. The Jewish pigs and Christian dogs cherish life, but we are indifferent to death. You are assured of rewards in paradise beyond your imagining."

Asfour reached under his chair and, with a thud, slapped an explosive vest down on the table.

⊷⊶

Frank's cell phone didn't work in Israel, so he placed the call from his hotel room. A woman's voice answered with the Hebrew word for yes.

"*Ken?*"

"Dahlia?"

"Yes." Background sounds told him she was driving.

"It's Frank DiRaimo."

"Frank! Are you in Washington?"

"No, I'm back in Israel. Tel Aviv. The Ministry of Tourism is taking me around the country for a week so I can do travel reporting."

"Will we see you? Gil and Nurit sometimes talk about you."

"I'm not sure. I work for a wire service, so I'll have to file almost daily, and the ministry has packed so much into my itinerary I'll be lucky to get my stories written."

"Where will you go?"

"Well, the first stop is Armageddon."

# CHAPTER FORTY

Frank and Arnie emerged from the car and approached the ruins. Uri found a large dressed stone in a shady spot. He sat on the boulder, lit a cigarette, unfolded a Hebrew tabloid, and read the soccer news.

"Har Megiddo is the hill of battles," Arnie said as they walked along, "so it's not surprising that the New Testament predicts that this is where the final battle will begin. The tel was occupied for thousands of years. It guards the largest pass between the Jezreel Valley," Arnie gestured toward the panorama to the east, "and the coastal plain.

"The route along the plain linked Egypt with Syria and Iraq. Megiddo is thought to be one of King Solomon's chariot cities, although some archaeologists dispute the dates."

Frank looked into the valley and was amazed by its beauty.

"And wait till you see the water system," Arnie said.

The tour guide led Frank into a cavernous ancient tunnel.

"All this was chiseled out of the rock by hand."

Frank ran his fingers across the grooves left by each blow of the hammer.

"Amazing," Frank said.

"This place had to be able to withstand a siege," Arnie said, "but the water source was a spring on the hillside outside the city walls. Through this tunnel, the defenders could reach the water undetected without leaving the protection of the fortress. The entrance to the spring was camouflaged."

"It boggles the mind," Frank said, astounded by the tunnel's capaciousness.

"I think Sepphoris, our next stop, will also surprise you."

At his home near Jenin, the suicide bomber and his mother smiled for the cameras. The woman wore a headscarf and traditional clothing. Her son wore a green headband inscribed with Arabic writing, his explosive vest, and he carried a Kalashnikov assault rifle. A dozen people moved about in front of the two, some ululating and some praising the glories of martyrdom. Flashes went off, and videographers angled for better positions.

The spectacular discoveries unearthed at Sepphoris put Frank, a historian with an interest in archaeology, in his element. He couldn't escape the delicious feeling that he was getting away with something. Here he was earning a salary, with all expenses paid, while living a dream. For one of the few times in his life, he didn't wish he were somewhere else. He was exactly where he wanted to be doing just what he wanted to do. How lucky, he thought.

"See that hill?" Arnie asked.

"I think I see the one you mean."

"That's Nazareth. Most people know Nazareth was a tiny village in Jesus' time, but they don't know that Sepphoris, an important city, stood here only four miles away. By tradition it's the hometown of Mary, Jesus' mother.

"When Jesus was a little boy, there was a revolt, and the Romans burned the city. But when Jesus was a young man, Herod Antipas rebuilt it. The construction here would have provided work for a family involved in the building trade.

"Later, after the Romans destroyed the Temple in Jerusalem, Sepphoris became the center of Jewish spiritual life. Yehuda ha-Nasi, who compiled the Mishna, lived here, and he relocated the Sanhedrin to Sepphoris."

Arnie led Frank to the ruins of a villa. The floor still was in good shape with the mosaics largely intact.

"My God! Look at her."

Frank had stopped above the mosaic portrait of a beautiful young woman.

"What a heartbreaker. Was she Jewish? Greek? Roman?"

"Use your imagination," said Arnie, smiling, "and you can't go wrong."

⸎ ⸎

Ahmed Asfour stood in the sun giving final instructions to his protégé.

"Remember to use your vest where you can kill as many Jews as possible."

⇌ ⇌

Frank and Arnie followed Boris, a young man who spoke English with a Russian accent, around the restoration of Nazareth as it would have appeared during Jesus' life. Lending atmosphere, Arab families in first-century garb tended sheep and goats.

Boris explained: "These are the crops of biblical times growing on the original hillside terraces: olives, almonds, grapes, wheat, barley, figs, and carob. And this wine press, carved into the rock, dates from Jesus' life here."

Frank sat on the rock into which the wine press had been carved and ran his fingers over the opening.

⇌ ⇌

The Border Policeman nudged his sergeant.

"What's that?" he asked, inclining his head toward a young man in the distance wearing a long, heavy coat in the warmth of the day. As the young man drew nearer, the gendarmes could see that he looked sweaty and nervous.

"Hey, you!" the sergeant shouted in Arabic.

The young man was noticeably startled.

"Come here!"

The bomber turned and bolted, leading the patrol on a chase into a cluster of buildings separated by narrow alleys. He gained some distance on the Border Police and vaulted over a wall, but his coat and suicide vest spoiled his timing, causing him to land badly and to turn his ankle. He hobbled off and found a hiding place in a tool shed. Panting, he watched the patrol run past through a crack in the slats.

# CHAPTER FORTY ONE

Frank met Arnie and Uri in the hotel coffee shop for breakfast.

"*Boker tov!*" Frank said, pleased that he now could say "good morning" in Hebrew.

"*Boker tov,*" said Arnie, with a mischievous look. How would you like to go off script today?"

"What do you mean?

"Depart from your itinerary. See some of Arab Israel. Strictly off the books, of course. Don't tell the Tourism Ministry, and you can't write about it, or I'll get fried."

"What do you have in mind?"

"Last night I ran into a tour guide I know in the lobby. She's an Arab Christian, and we've worked together before. I mentioned that I'm guiding an open-minded American, and I asked what she was up to. She was going to take a French couple to a Muslim wedding near here today, but they backed out. She asked if we'd like to go instead."

"Would we be welcome?"

"She seems to think it would be OK. You'd have to pay her for a day's work. She's reasonable. Do you think you'd want to do that?"

"I should be able to swing it if you take me to an ATM."

Of course, it would mean skipping the Bahai Temple in Haifa."

"Deal!"

*⟢ ⟣*

"The two big clans in this part of the Galilee are feuding," said Fawzia, a petite woman with delicate features and auburn hair. Through the back window she spoke in Arabic to one of the armed guards at the compound's entrance. He waved them through. Cars were everywhere, but Uri found a place to park that Frank would have missed. Frank got out and looked up. On rooftops, gunmen with Kalashnikovs had positioned themselves to deliver enfilade fire. This is like the Corleone family, Frank thought.

On three sides, a cluster of lavish, multi-storied homes bordered a large open space where hundreds of men milled about, renewing old acquaintances and catching up on events.

"Where are the women?" Frank asked, feeling cheated.

"They're in the back," Fawzia said. "You won't see them."

"The bride too?"

"The bride especially," Arnie said. "This is a traditional family."

Frank grunted.

"Fawzia will be the only woman here," Arnie said.

"There's Sheikh Khaled!" Fawzia said, excusing herself.

"He's the clan leader and father of the groom," Arnie told Frank.

Fawzia waited at a respectful distance until the patriarch concluded his conversation with a portly guest in a bespoke suit that was quite a departure from the leisurewear favored by Jewish Israelis. Fawzia and her host conversed for a moment and then joined Frank, Arnie, and Uri.

"Sheikh Khaled," Fawzia said, "May I present Mr. DiRaimo, a visitor from the United States."

"You are welcome here," said the sheikh with a smile. He was a trim, handsome man who reminded Frank a little of David Niven. Frank noticed that most of the senior men had mustaches.

"And this is my colleague Arnie Mehlman and his associate Uri Gabay."

"Nice to see you," said the sheik with a nod of the head. "I hope you will make yourselves at home." Then he was off, greeting other guests.

Frank remembered the words of a British officer in Mandatory Palestine. "At least the Arabs pretend they're happy to see you," he wrote, making an unfavorable comparison with the Jews.

The distant sound of automatic gunfire seized Frank's attention, but no one else paid it much heed.

"What's that?" he asked.

"Oh, there are other weddings around here today," Fawzia said. "People shoot into the air to celebrate."

A young man walked up. "Good afternoon," he said with a smile and a nod. Then he spoke to Fawzia in Arabic.

"This is Fadl," she explained. "Sheikh Khaled asked him to stay with us to make sure we have everything we need. He speaks English."

Frank heard the slap of a palm on a drum and the tap of a fingertip on a microphone. Across the crowded plaza, entertainers were setting up the sound system. Two percussionists held drums of different design. A violinist bowed a note to a lute player who turned a tuning peg.

Frank asked Fawzia the name of a large flat stringed instrument that sat on the lap of a musician who plucked test notes with finger picks.

"That's a *kanun*," she said. "How do you say it in English? Maybe it's like a zither."

The music began, and the guests drifted toward seats set up in a large U facing the entertainers. A man sang into the microphone, and two boys brandishing knives performed a daring dance. The music sent a charge through the crowd, transforming it in moments into a single organism. Hypnotic drumming filled the air. Masterfully, the singer dominated the space.

"He's improvising!" Fawzia exclaimed. "That's not a traditional song. He's making it up as he goes along especially for Sheikh Khaled and his family. Gee, he's good. What talent."

Because Frank and the others had more or less invited themselves, they didn't assume chairs set out for the guests. Rather, they stood behind men seated at the base of the U. Suddenly, a well-dressed man in front of Frank leaped to his feet, held a bloody wrist in the air with his uninjured hand and, with a fierce expression, said something in Arabic.

"Sniper! Sniper!" cried Fadl.

Everyone scattered. In a crouch, Frank scrambled after Fadl and found himself in a long entrance hall where cushions lined the walls. He cursed himself as a coward for losing sight of Fawzia, but what could he do now? By this time she would have found her own spot.

Two gunmen burst into the room pushing a terrified boy of about 13. Frank couldn't understand what they were saying, and this was no time to ask intrusive questions, but it seemed clear that the boy was being accused of spotting for the sniper. The gunmen bristled with the potential of instant violence, and Frank was afraid they would kill their captive then and there. The boy hunkered on his heels, trembling, his eyes beseeching salvation. Long minutes passed. The men with Kalashnikovs took no notice of Frank. If they decided to execute the boy, the presence of a Westerner would not inhibit them. A man appeared at the entrance and delivered a short message.

"Clear," Fadl announced.

Slowly, Frank got to his feet. With toxic glances back to the boy, the gunmen walked out. Frank looked with puzzlement at Fadl, who shrugged.

In the courtyard, Fawzia, Arnie, and Uri could have been discussing the weather. The gunshot victim sat nearby having his wrist bandaged. He resembled Gilbert Roland, a Mexican-American movie actor Frank had admired as a boy, but taller and more intimidating.

"The doctor thinks it probably wasn't a sniper," Fawzia informed Frank. "More likely the bullet was shot in the air and fell here."

If it had been a sniper, Frank realized, the bullet would have passed between Fawzia and himself. As it was, it dropped a few feet in front of them.

The entertainment resumed, and the boys with the flashing knives danced even more audaciously to the beat of the drums. Fawzia, with a serene countenance, swayed demurely in place. The incident didn't seem to have troubled her at all. Frank stole a glance at Arnie, who looked back at him sheepishly. Frank rolled his eyes in a silent signal of understanding. Arnie was safe. Frank wouldn't report him to the Tourism Ministry.

"That's Hassan, the groom," Fawzia said, pointing out a young man with boyish good looks and a kind face.

Off to the left, retainers put the finishing touches on long tables laden with food. When it came time to eat, Frank and the others hung back. After all, they were there as spectators, not for a free meal. But after the line thinned, Hassan approached Frank, took him gently by the sleeve, and led him to the buffet. With a movement of his head, Hassan invited the others to follow.

What a feast! Frank couldn't recall such a spread, superlative in quality and quantity. Fresh ingredients and subtle spices set even the ordinary dishes apart. The salads, hummus, tabouli, babaganoush, and dolma all were outstanding. The broiled chicken was the best Frank had ever eaten. What was the secret? He sampled kebab in tomato sauce, roasted cauliflower, shawarma, stuffed lamb shoulder, and various delicacies flavored with dried lemon. He passed up the pastries in favor of saffron rice with cashews and raisins topped with date compote.

"Can you guys still walk?" Frank asked Arnie and Uri.

"*Metzuyan,*" said Uri, who was not entirely at ease in English.

"He says it's excellent," Arnie translated. Arnie pulled Frank aside and whispered in his ear. "I wasn't sure Uri would eat any of this because it isn't kosher. Another secret to keep."

"Safe with me," Frank said.

"Mr. DiRaimo." It was Fadl. "The sheikh would like a word with you, if you don't mind."

"Of course."

"He's asked me to interpret," Fadl said as they walked toward the largest of the houses. "His English is good, but he's more comfortable in Arabic."

Sheikh Khaled stood in the courtyard flanked by two serious looking gentlemen in suits. He seemed happy to see Frank and spoke in Arabic.

"He says he's honored that you were able to be his guest today and would like to know if you can join him for coffee."

Frank didn't want coffee that late in the day, but he knew it would be an insult to refuse. And he burned with curiosity to learn more.

"You are very kind," said Frank.

The Arabs insisted that Frank enter the dwelling first, and he found himself in a long antechamber similar to the one in which he had taken refuge two hours before. This one, however, had furniture along the walls as well as cushions and small tables every few meters. Khaled took his place at the end of the room, facing the entrance, and Frank was seated in an upholstered chair at his side.

A man entered carrying a tray with a brass coffeepot and a set of small ceramic cups without handles. The pot intrigued Frank. It looked very old and had a pleasing dull patina. It was wider at the base and the top than in the middle, and two lines of tasteful engraving were inscribed around the rim. The spout was like the beak of a giant hawk, and the handle – gracefully curving along the pot's length – was secured with handcrafted rivets. The cups were adorned in an understated pattern of gold leaf. Frank admired the sheikh's elegant taste, which included nothing gaudy, ostentatious or ornate.

Frank studied the epicene body language of the man who poured the coffee. The server averted his eyes as he distributed the cups, and his diffident movements seemed to indicate an awareness that he was of lower status than the men who sat with the clan leader.

Frank sipped the steaming beverage, trying not to burn his mouth. The coffee had an unusual flavor. Was it cardamom?

The sheikh spoke in Arabic and Fadl translated back and forth.

"What part of the United States are you from?" Khaled asked.

"Washington, DC, the capital city."

"And how long will you be here?"

"In Israel? Only a few more days."

"You look to me like a man of respect. I believe you respect me -- "

"Yes, of course!"

"And I respect you. We're about the same age."

"Yes."

"It would be a pleasure to see you again." The sheikh looked at Frank with a playful expression. "Perhaps you will bring me a beautiful American woman, and I will give you a beautiful Arab woman."

Frank's countenance brightened at the sheer exotic insanity of it all. Was he serious?

"Yes, maybe we can do that," Frank said, laughing.

⊫╬ ╬⊨

They rode along in silence. Frank decided not to tell the others about the gunmen and the boy. He didn't want Arnie to regret having suggested the change in plans. Frank looked to his left at Uri, driving impassively. Straining against his seatbelt, he turned to Fawzia and Arnie in the back.

"I suppose you're wondering what Sheikh Khaled had to say."

"Yes!" they cried out in unison.

"He wanted to swap women with me."

"That's very tribal!" Fawzia said with open admiration.

"Was he joking?" Arnie asked.

"I don't know. Fawzia, what do you think?"

"Not completely joking. He left the door open for you to take it either way. It's within his tradition, and it was the custom not that long ago. He seems to have taken a liking to you."

Frank flexed his arms at the elbows, leaned back in his seat, and stretched contentedly.

"This beats the hell out of the Bahai Temple," he said.

# CHAPTER FORTY TWO

The fragrance of flowering citrus greeted them as they approached Kibbutz Ginosar. To Frank it was the sweetest and most enchanting scent in the world.

"What a wonderful smell! What fruit is that?" Frank asked.

"Grapefruit," Arnie said.

They drove past a grove in which each plant was shrouded in plastic at the place where the stalk met the branches. "And here's where we grow plastic bags," Arnie said. "Just kidding. They're bananas. Over there is Lake Kinneret – the Sea of Galilee."

"This place is *nice*," Frank said.

"A lot of the kibbutzim are turning into family friendly resorts," Arnie said. "You can let the kids play and not worry about them."

"You're Catholic, right?" Arnie asked.

"Raised."

"Remember Mary Magdalene?"

"How could I forget?"

"The ancient town of Migdal was just a few hundred meters south of here. The name means 'tower.' Most sources say that Migdal was Miriam's hometown, and that's why she came to be called the Magdalene."

The car pulled into the parking lot. Frank, Arnie, and Uri got out and walked toward the main building for check-in.

"Tonight we'll eat Shabbat dinner in the guest house," Arnie said, "and in the morning you'll see the 'Jesus boat.' "

That evening the dining hall was filled almost to overflowing. This was just enough people for Frank's taste. Although it was a large gathering, there was no waiting or crowding. Ascending the stairs to the second deck, Frank found himself directly behind a tall, elegant Ashkenazi woman. Her silver-blonde hair, which appeared to be natural, was plaited into a French braid and twisted into a topknot. As she turned to speak to a companion, her exquisite profile came into view. I wonder if she's married, Frank thought. Probably so. Women like that don't wander around loose for long. He tried not to be too obvious about looking at her.

In the dining room Frank picked up his tray, craning his neck so as not to lose sight of the woman as she merged into the crowd. Yes, there was a man who appeared to be her husband. He looked like a nice guy. No envy! No envy! Frank reminded himself. Bless them both. God grant them a long and happy life together. Of the Seven Deadly Sins, Frank considered only envy to be unworthy of him. Lust, gluttony, greed, sloth, wrath and pride might be regrettable, but Frank wasn't ashamed of these failings. Envy, however, was for losers.

Frank, Arnie, and Uri filled their trays, selecting from an abundance of delicious foods, both hot and cold. At dinner the three briefly discussed *ha matzav*, Hebrew for "the situation," shorthand for the terror onslaught that Frank believed to be a war brought on by the Oslo Agreements. Just today there had been an explosion in Jerusalem.

"They can make us bleed," Arnie said, "but they can't drive us out."

After dinner Frank walked by himself on the shore of the Sea of Galilee. What a thrill to be there! This trip was turning out to be one of the highlights of his life. He watched the lake turn dark as the sun set behind him.

The museum the next morning was all he could have hoped for.

"In 1986 two brothers from the kibbutz discovered this ancient boat in the lake bottom," said the well-favored blonde with a slight Dutch accent. "It was exposed by a drought. Carbon 14 tests, the manner of its construction, and an oil lamp found in the boat all place it at the time of Jesus."

"Amazing!" Frank said.

"Sediment was all that preserved the wood," the guide continued. "Excavators packed the hull in fiberglass foam and floated it here, where it underwent an 11-year-long conservation process in a specially built pool. The boat was submerged in a solution of synthetic wax, which gradually replaced the water in the wood cells."

Frank walked around the 2,000-year-old vessel, examining it from all angles.

"It brings religion and history to life," he said.

⊫⊪ ⊪⊫

At the safe house near Jenin, Ahmed Asfour wrapped an elastic bandage around the suicide bomber's ankle.

⊫⊪ ⊪⊫

Frank, Arni, and Uri were enjoying lunch at a beachfront hotel in Tel Aviv, when Frank spotted someone he recognized a few tables away. It was Peter Lyle, a British journalist. Their paths had crossed at Consolidated Press before Lyle had accepted an offer from a left-wing British paper.

"That's someone I know," Frank said. "Excuse me, please."

The Englishman sat alone reading a newspaper, smoking a cigarette, a cup of coffee before him.

"Peter!"

Lyle looked up without a change of expression.

"DiRaimo." Lyle limply accepted Frank's proffered handshake. "Are you still with Consolidated Press?"

"Still. I'd heard you'd become The Sentinel's Mideast correspondent."

"Yes. Are you covering the intifada?"

"No," said Frank, a little embarrassed. "Travel writing. The Ministry of Tourism is paying for it."

"And are those your Mossad handlers over there? Careful you don't get spun, Frank."

"I can't even get them to talk politics."

"Just as well, now that you're in the pay of the Israeli government."

"My copy will have to speak for itself. Are you doing anything analytical?"

"As a matter of fact, I'm beginning a series on the next generation of likely Palestinian leaders."

"Interesting angle."

"But covering the resistance keeps me pretty busy."

"Resistance?" said Frank, suddenly cool. "Is that what you call it?"

"Of course. An indigenous people's legitimate resistance against colonial occupation."

"Oh, come on!"

"Occupied Arab land."

"Spain is occupied Arab land, and we're not giving that back. Besides, the PLO was trying to destroy Israel before there was any occupation, and the Palestinian Authority would continue to do so even if Israel withdrew from the territories unilaterally. What about the Syrian occupation of Lebanon? I'm sure you're not too worked up over that. And while we're on the subject of Arab occupation, when the Egyptians ruled Gaza and the Jordanians ruled the West Bank, they showed no signs of giving their Arab 'brethren' a state."

"That's a remarkably unsophisticated analysis even from an American. Israel is a Western colony in the heart of the Arab world. Like any foreign body, it generates inflammation. I would think at least you would recognize that every dispute has two sides."

"The other side always has a case. Hitler had a case. He had reason to be angry about the Treaty of Versailles. You can go around and around forever about who's right. In the end it matters less who's right than whose side you're on. Take it easy, Peter."

Frank turned and rejoined his companions.

# CHAPTER FORTY THREE

H e couldn't believe the scene on the plane. The flight
was filling up, and three passengers had taken their
seats two rows in front of him -- an ultra-Orthodox man in
full regalia and what appeared to be a secular husband and
wife. The haredi had the aisle seat, the husband the middle,
and the wife sat by the window. But as the aircraft was about to
taxi for takeoff, the husband decided he wanted the window
seat. An acrobatic switch ensued in the cramped space, with
arched backs, pelvic tilts, obtruding rumps, and heads bump-
ing against the luggage bins. The cabin was warm, and during
these contortions the woman shed her cardigan, leaving her
in a sleeveless top.

The haredi pitched a fit. He jumped into the aisle and
shouted that he would not sit next to the woman. The stewardess couldn't calm him or get him to relent. The husband, now
indignant, refused to return to the middle seat, so the pilot

couldn't move the plane. It would have done no good for Frank
to offer to switch seats because a woman sat to his right. Finally,
a passenger came forward and assumed the seat, vacating a
spot between two men where the haredi was willing to sit. But
by this time, the flight had lost its assigned place in the takeoff
sequence and was dropped to the bottom of the queue.

"For this we need a Jewish state?" Frank said aloud. He
didn't care who heard. When in high school, he had become
enamored of the idea of the sinewy, sun-bronzed, secular
Israeli – a farmer-soldier akin to those of the Roman re-
public -- as the antithesis of the ghetto Jew. Soon thereafter,
Paul Newman -- romantically entwined with über-Aryan Eva
Marie Saint -- embodied this ideal on the screen. In the final scene of "Exodus," rifles in hand, Paul and Eva Marie
roar off together in a truck, about to do battle for Israel's
independence.

Now this pasty putz with beard dandruff doesn't fight and
won't sit next to a woman. How far have we sunk? Send him
back to the shtetl and let him wait for his moshiach there. Let
him take his chances with the Cossacks. And ugly! What anti-
Semite designed that outfit and forced him to wear it?

The delay almost caused Frank to miss his connecting
flight from New York to Washington, which caused him anxi-
ety and irritated him further. But it also made him especially
happy to be met by Janet at the airport. Once again, he was
in her debt.

※+ +※

Tobias Moore stood above Frank's cubicle in the
Consolidated Press newsroom.

"Good stories, Frank. I've talked with Tom. He thinks we should let you write features for awhile and give Paul a chance over at the State Department."

"Great!" Frank said.

⊨⊨

Frank went out his front door to fetch the morning papers. He bent to pick them up, and as he rose a headline caught his attention: "Attacks Against Israelis Mount: Settler children gunned down in West Bank trailer."

He swallowed hard, turned, and reentered the townhouse.

⊨⊨

In his cubicle at work, Frank typed "volunteers" and "Israel" into the search engine. He opened the first entry and read: "Welcome to Sar El, the national project for Volunteers for Israel."

He smiled.

⊨⊨

Frank dialed the number of Don's student apartment in Minnesota.

"Hello," Don said.

"Hi. It's Dad."

"Oh, hi."

From background sounds, Frank could tell that Don had been watching a ball game on TV. As the sounds receded,

Frank could picture Don picking up the remote and lowering the volume while continuing to watch the game.

"How are things?" Frank asked.

"Well, not so good."

"What's wrong?"

"I lost my scholarship."

"Lost your scholarship? If I had known you were having trouble, I could have got you a tutor. You should have told -- "

"It's not my grades. I quit the team."

"Why?"

"The coach yelled at me."

"The coach yelled at you? That's no reason to quit. That's what coaches *do!* And I can't afford to pay full tuition."

"I'll think of something."

"Look. I went to graduate school on the GI Bill. My father did his surgical residency on the GI Bill. Why don't you finish up the semester and then take a break from school and do a hitch in the armed forces? Then when you get out -- "

"I'm not going to do that, and I'm tired of you trying to tell me what to do."

"I'm your father. Who's supposed to tell -- ?"

"You weren't there when we were growing up."

"So what am I, a stranger? I've talked more to you on the phone than my father spoke to me in person."

"Yes, but those calls were more for you than for me."

Frank inhaled sharply, assailed equally by guilt and resentment.

"Listen. This is why I called today. And I hope it's for you as well as for me. I would have been thrilled if my Dad had come up with an idea like this."

"Like what?"

"Come to Israel with me when the semester ends. You know, they're getting hammered over there. There's a program where you spend three weeks as a civilian volunteer with the Israeli Army. It's non-combat service, but it saves them the cost of calling up a reservist."

"Where would you get the money for a trip like that?

"My mother sold some stock and gave a few thousand dollars to each of her children. Plus I should get a small tax refund."

"I'm not interested," said Don, adding: "You should get all the rich Jews to pay for it."

Frank was shocked and hurt.

"Where do you hear talk like that?" he asked his son.

Frank hoped he would have better luck with his daughter. Before calling her he walked along the Potomac to calm down and clear his mind.

"Hello," Laura said.

"Hi, doll."

"Oh. Hi, Dad."

"How are you doing?"

"Pretty good."

"What are you up to?"

"Folding laundry."

"How are your classes going?'

"Not bad, I think."

"That's good. Say, I've got an idea. Tell me what you think. You know, the Israelis are under attack. The Arabs are blowing up restaurants and shooting kids in their bedrooms. I'm going over to volunteer for a few weeks on an army base. I was hoping that you and Don and I could go together, but he's not interested. What do you say?"

"It's not my fight."

"Oh."

"Are you looking for a new family, Dad? People who will feel grateful to you?

"You always knew how to slice me up. But what difference does it make what I'm looking for? Suppose my motives – deep down, where even I can't see them – stink. Those people still deserve our help."

Laura said nothing.

"You know, Don says I shouldn't give him advice because I wasn't there when you two were growing up."

"What do you expect?" Laura said.

# CHAPTER FORTY FOUR

Frank caught Tobias Moore's attention as the international editor walked by his cubicle.

"Tobias. Would it be OK if I take a few weeks of vacation?"

"Sure. You've earned it. Where are you going?"

"Israel."

Moore's face betrayed a flash of revulsion.

"Why?"

"To show solidarity."

"For which side?" Moore asked softly, with a hint of menace.

"Come on, Tobias. You know which side. The Israelis."

Moore furrowed his brow.

"I had no idea you were such a Zionist. Where in Israel will you be going?"

"Wherever they send me."

≈⊰ ⊱≈

Frank sat across from the desk of Executive Editor Tom Sheridan.

"If you put on an IDF uniform, you will have crossed a line," Sheridan said. "You can never write for us about the Middle East again, and we can't send you back to the State Department. You will have limited your use to this organization."

"Tom, you know as well as I do that the whole idea of a neutral press is bogus. Was Edward R. Murrow neutral during the Blitz? Everyone has a point of view. The only defense against accusations of bias is to say: 'Show me what's wrong with the story.' That's the kind of backup I expect from you. When I return I'll be writing the same kinds of stories I've always written, and it's up to the company to protect me from personal attacks."

"The company really doesn't want you to make this trip, Frank."

Silence.

"I'll think about what you've said."

≈⊰ ⊱≈

Janet poured herself a drink from a wine bottle.

"I've decided not to cancel my trip," Frank said.

Her eyes flashed with anger.

"Frank, you're old enough to stop being reckless. Think about it. You're well into your 50s. Jobs in journalism are hard to come by, especially in Washington. If you want to change jobs, it's better to do it from a position of strength. Nobody wants to hire the unemployed. They want to steal good people away from the competition. You need to be realistic."

Janet took a long swallow.

"I am being realistic," Frank said. "I know I'm not good at hiding my feelings. If I go, they'll get over it. If I let them bully me into not going, I *won't* get over it. And it will show on my face. I'm more likely to be fired if I cancel the trip and resent my bosses forever than if I go and they're annoyed with me for awhile."

"You're being a jerk! Why are you doing this? Do you have a kamikaze complex? Do you expect me to support you when you lose your job? Look. The Jews need to accept the fact that Israel is a failed experiment. It's a graft that didn't take. What's the solution to all this fighting? For them to keep killing more Arabs?"

"The Israelis have nowhere else to go."

"Let them come here. Give them Idaho!"

"The Jews have more right to Israel than my grandparents had to America. European settlers did a lot worse things to the Indians than the Jews ever did to the Arabs, but that doesn't mean I'm going back to Italy. Israelis have a right to Israel for the same reason Americans have a right to the United States – because they built it, and what you create is yours."

"It's not the same. The Jews got to Palestine too late."

"It's the same as it's always been. There are no 'immaculate conceptions' of new nations. All were born in sin, and all territories were laid claim to at one time or another – even if some were claimed a long time ago."

"History changes!"

"No it doesn't. At the same time Israel was fighting for its existence, millions of ethnic Germans were expelled from their ancestral homes in Czechoslovakia and Poland, and nobody said boo. They'd been there a lot longer than most of the Arabs have lived in Palestine. Does that mean German teenagers should be blowing up buses in Breslau?"

"But the Israelis are so outnumbered, the only way they can survive is to keep killing more and more Arabs. Is that your 'Final Solution' to the Mideast problem?"

"You want a neat ending, and real life doesn't have endings. It just goes on. Sometimes the best you can do is to endure and to wait for opportunities as they arise."

Janet drained her glass. It was clear that she would kill the bottle this evening. Her voice took on an angry edge.

"How can you tell an Arab born in the town of his great-grandparents that he has to make way for an immigrant from Russia or Brooklyn? You can't kick people out of a place just because your ancestors might have lived there 2,000 years ago."

"In the end it's not about policy," Frank said sadly. "It's about love. It's a matter of who you love and who you don't. Simple as that."

"Sometimes I think you love only Israel," Janet said. She took another drink. "You don't even love yourself. Nothing will ever be enough for you. You're a bottomless pit. You'll always want more, more, more."

She poured the last drops from the bottle. "I'm not anti-Semitic."

"Sure."

"I just hate -- "

"That's what they all say."

"How will you get to the airport?"

"I'll take a cab."

PART FIVE

# CHAPTER FORTY FIVE

Zero one one. Nine seven two. Frank entered Dahlia's number on the keypad. He was calling first thing in the morning, still early afternoon in Israel.

"*Ken?*"

"Dahlia? It's Frank DiRaimo. Listen. I'm coming to Israel, and this time I don't want to miss you."

"Very good. Are you writing stories?"

"No. Not reporting. I'm coming as a Sar El volunteer."

"Fantastic! My parents in Herzliya sometimes host volunteers for the weekend. Where are they sending you?"

"I won't know till I get there. I'll call from the base a few days after I arrive."

"It will be good to see you."

After the derogation by Janet and his children, the simple words of acceptance caught Frank by surprise. Tears filled his eyes, and he choked up, but he didn't want Dahlia to hear him sob.

"Yes, and you too," he said quickly. "Bye."

"Bye for now," Dahlia said. *"Lehitraot."*

⇥ ⇤

One evening after work, Frank parked behind the ancient Cadillac in the old man's driveway. He straightened his tie at the door and rang the bell. Soon he heard faint sounds inside, and the door opened.

"So you're one of those I spoke to at The Washington Times?'

"Yes."

Fritz Kraemer now was almost 94 and frail, but the piercing eyes and fierce visage were unchanged. One of a kind, Frank thought. The real deal. Although Kraemer never was a large man, at the end of his life his personage still was larger than life. Frank felt himself to be in the presence of greatness.

"Come in," Kraemer said. The old man took a seat in a simple chair opposite the front door.

"Do you have a recording device?"

"No."

"Come here!"

Kraemer patted Frank down under his suit jacket for a wire.

"Come into the living room. So you want to talk to me about geo-strategy."

Kraemer's reputation as a monarchist did not prevent Frank's surprise at seeing a small, framed photograph of Kaiser Wilhelm II. The austere front room with its simple furnishings looked like it had been last decorated during the Truman administration.

"Yes, among other things."

"Other things? Are you writing a story?"

"No. This is for my own benefit."

"I thought you wanted my analysis of the attacks last September."

"That was my original intent, and I'd like to get to it. But now I have a more urgent matter to discuss."

"If I'm going to talk with you, I must know who you are. Tell me your background."

Frank quickly summarized his life: college, Vietnam, graduate school, teaching, more graduate school, more teaching, journalism.

Kraemer noted Frank's Vietnam service with interest and approval. For one of the few times in his life, Frank received appreciation for this rather than scorn, indifference, or pity. He had passed one of Kraemer's exacting tests. So far, so good.

"What is this 'more urgent matter'?"

"I want to be a civilian volunteer for three weeks with the Israeli Army, but my boss doesn't want me to go, my woman friend opposes it, and my two kids in college think I'm being selfish."

"Everything's blowing up over there. Why do you want to go?"

"*Warum nicht?* Why isn't everyone going?"

"Ah, I see," said Kraemer, looking at Frank as if for the first time. "And you want my opinion as to whether you should go?"

"No. I'm going in any case."

"So you're like Kissinger!" he roared. "You don't come to me for advice. You come for absolution!"

"Something like that."

Frank knew that mentor and protégé had not spoken for almost 30 years. Kraemer cut off contact after Kissinger had signed the pact that sealed the fate of South Vietnam.

Kraemer's face softened.

"I'm going to tell you some things. Maybe you know them, maybe you don't. Perhaps you can benefit from a review. First, you're not ten a penny."

Although Frank was unfamiliar with the expression, he grasped its meaning instantly. But he put on a quizzical expression to coax more information out of Kraemer.

"You're unusual. Not run of the mill. Apart from the herd. But this comes at a cost. Being different isn't enough. If you are true to your convictions, if you are to be a man of character, you must accept that loneliness is the price of excellence. Exceptional people are exceptionally lonely. You will stand apart even from those closest to you."

Frank silently took this in.

"You must understand the motives of the people around you as well as those of your enemies. The people you see every day are willfully blind. This comes from fear and avoidance. Our bourgeois society is a coward at heart. Unlike you, the bourgeois is not a risk-taker. He cannot recognize the threat posed by a few determined fanatics who are willing to fight even though they know they will lose – people like those who flew airplanes into our buildings."

"Or those who strap bombs to themselves and explode in Israeli restaurants," Frank said.

Was that a small smile of satisfaction? Frank wasn't sure.

"The bourgeois does not recognize such threats," Kraemer said, "because the danger originates in a setting outside his experience – a context of which he knows nothing, one he cannot even envisage. The bourgeois cannot imagine that anyone could be so wild and determined. He can't understand that riders of the apocalypse fight to the bitter end. And when cornered, fanatics always believe that a miracle still could save them."

Kraemer spoke quickly, packing content into few words. The old man is distilling his curriculum, Frank thought, knowing he has little time left on Earth. Frank wondered if he would be Kraemer's last student and felt honored by the possibility.

"The wicked can be courageous," Kraemer went on. "Courage for a bad cause is just as effective as courage for a good one. To fanatics, heroism means fighting for a hopeless cause. The bourgeois does not understand this kind of thinking.

"In the better social circles these days, one may not remark that physical cowardice is a vice," Kraemer said. "Overly civilized people who become excessively intellectual won't fight. When the bourgeois fears for his existence, he has only one wish: acquiescence to the power that threatens him. You've heard of the fight-or-flight response, but the actual sequence is fight-or-flight, freezing in place, and then fawning supplication. And all this can happen in seconds!"

"That explains why so many are ready to throw Israel to the wolves, especially in Europe," Frank said. "The more Jews killed, the more unpopular Jews become."

"We must protect allies or no one will have any confidence in the United States," Kraemer said. "For years after Vietnam, we lost credibility around the world."

"The Israelis protect themselves," Frank said, "but we can give moral support. My presence will free a soldier to patrol for a few weeks."

"If you look at it objectively," Kraemer said, "plain violence and raw power are necessary to check wild, untamed fanatics. But our bourgeois society does not believe in power pure and simple. It believes in World Public Opinion. The bourgeois rationalist is disinclined to believe in the importance of intangible factors. He doesn't recognize that the soul plays an important part in the foreign and security policies of states and alliances. Even Kissinger has never fully accepted this! Therefore, he's treated Israel soullessly -- as a pawn in a greater game. But you grasp these things instinctively, don't you?"

"Yes."

"And that's why you will always be lonely."

# CHAPTER FORTY SIX

Frank emerged from customs and immigration and dragged his bags to the Information Desk.

"Sar El?" said the pleasant looking woman behind the desk. "Your *madricha* will be around to pick you up. Would you like a cup of tea while you're waiting?"

"Yes, that would be nice."

To keep his luggage from blocking the desk, Frank moved his bags against a wall about 20 feet away and waited there while the tea was brewing. When the woman reappeared with his tea, he walked back to the desk, leaving his bags unattended.

"Thank you," said Frank, accepting the cup.

"Excuse me, sir. Are those your bags?"

It was one of two shaven-headed young security men.

"Yes," said Frank, embarrassed. "So sorry." Hardly a minute had elapsed since he had crossed the hall.

Reunited with his bags, Frank blew on the surface of the hot tea and sipped. A pretty young soldier with opal eyes approached with a clipboard.

"Shalom. I'm Anna, your *madricha*. You are -- ?"

"Frank DiRaimo."

Anna checked his name off a list.

"This way, please." Was that a slight Russian accent?

Frank put the cup down on the Information Desk. He smiled at the woman who had given him the tea and waved goodbye, then he grabbed his bags and followed Anna to the main terminal area, where most of the volunteers in his group had gathered. After some self-introductions, bustle, and small talk, the volunteers were loaded onto a bus.

Many got their first look at Israel through the windows. Others pointed out places they recognized.

After a stop at another base where about a third of the passengers were let off, the bus rolled through the main gate of the sprawling Tel HaShomer army post. They passed the Sheba Medical Center and a field of parked Merkava tanks before arriving at Matzrap, a shabby warehouse district where the Israel Defense Forces' medical supplies were received, sorted and distributed.

The volunteers disembarked and retrieved their bags from the lower compartment. Following Anna's instructions, Frank took his things to one of the men's barracks rooms. Holy shit! Eight guys in this tiny space? Frank had forgotten how much smaller and closer together everything is in Israel. He knew it would be Spartan, communal living, but he had pictured a squad bay or a capacious Quonset hut similar to those he had inhabited in the Army. Those domed huts had leeway between the cots, but here four bunk beds were crammed into one small hutch. The window air conditioner rattled dispiritedly. It clearly wasn't working right. The stuffy room wasn't much cooler than the baking parade ground, and no other window could be opened for ventilation.

Frank threw a duffle bag on one of the lower cots. He wanted no acrobatics when he got up in the middle of the night to go to the latrine. Let one of the agile, younger guys with a smaller prostate sleep topside.

After the volunteers had unpacked and stowed their belongings into lockers, Anna lined them up in the scorching sun and ushered them to a warehouse where they were issued uniforms. The shirt and trousers Frank received looked like remnants from the 1956 Sinai campaign. The boots and cap appeared to be a little newer.

"Back in uniform after 32 years," Frank said. But it had been even longer for some of the older men. A few were Korean War veterans, and Martin -- a trim 80-year-old – was a veteran of World War II.

In the chow line that evening, Frank stood behind Davida, an attractive woman from New Hampshire in her early 40s, and her 14-year-old daughter, Linda.

"We never were in Israel until Linda's bat mitzvah last year," Davida explained to Martin. "Even then I really didn't feel like coming. I was indifferent. I wasn't a second-class citizen in America. No one mistreated me. But when I got here, everything changed.

"I remember looking down and seeing the Lion of Judah on a sewer grate and thinking: This is for me. I'm not a minority here."

Davida noticed Frank listening intently.

"Was it the same for you?" she asked him.

"I'm not Jewish, so that's not an issue for me. But I've been a Zionist since I was 14 years old. I've just always identified with these people. Judaism is a pillar of Western civilization, and I'm of the West. Besides, I like Jews with guns."

A striking brunette walked past carrying a short-barreled M-16. Her uniform pants were tailored to show her derriere to great advantage.

"Especially Jewish girls with guns," Frank said to general laughter.

Inside the chow hall, Frank and the others picked up their trays and served themselves.

"Breakfast and supper are dairy meals," Martin explained. "The midday meal is heaviest and has meat."

With eggs, yogurt, and hummus among the supper offerings, Frank didn't feel deprived of protein.

In his bunk that night, Frank had trouble sleeping as the other men snored in the stuffy, crowded room. He had been right. The air conditioner wasn't working properly.

After breakfast, without much supervision, the volunteers wandered into the work areas where they would spend the next three weeks. Almost randomly, Frank ended up in a warehouse full of medical supplies partnered with Harriet, a 70-year-old woman from Brooklyn. Jet-lagged, Frank sat before a small table in a cheap plastic chair and received instructions from Rafi, a young reserve soldier of Moroccan origin, who interpreted for Simcha, the diminutive, bearded warehouse supervisor in a skullcap.

Simcha said something in Hebrew.

"He says to make sure the dates aren't expired," Rafi explained. "Pack the units 20 each into these plastic bags. Mark

20 on the bags, then put the bags into the cartons and mark on the cartons how many bags of 20 are inside."

Frank and Harriet set to work: one, two, three . . .

When two cartons were filled, Frank dragged them over to Rafi, who taped them shut, loaded them onto a hand truck, and rolled them off.

Harriet held open a plastic bag into which Frank dropped units of tubing.

"Eighteen, nineteen, twenty," he counted.

Harriet stapled the bag shut, marked it, and dropped it into the carton.

"This bag has 17 more," Frank said. "We're almost finished with the tubing." He looked around. "I wonder where Rafi went." Frank decided to address Simcha directly. Some Israelis knew more English than they were willing to let on.

"What's next?" Frank asked.

Simcha said something in Hebrew the Americans didn't understand. The second time he enunciated it more clearly, but Harriet and Frank still were bewildered. Simcha repeated his words for a third time, louder, more slowly and emphatically. Frank and Harriet looked at each other uncomprehendingly.

"I guess we'd better just finish this up," Frank said.

Harriet held open the bag.

"Eighteen, nineteen, *zwanzig!*"

"*Zwanzig?*" Simcha said. "*Ich war hier geboren, aber meine Eltern in Polen geboren waren.*"

Frank thought he had found a way of communicating with Simcha. In Rafi's absence, he would ask Simcha for direction in his elementary German. Simcha seemed to understand, but the supervisor never spoke anything but Hebrew in the presence of the volunteers again.

The work was boring, but in the course of the three weeks Frank enjoyed getting to know his counterparts. Unlike his colleagues in journalism and the professorate, he felt at home with them. Most were North Americans, but others came from all over the developed world. He guessed that between 20 percent and 25 percent were not Jewish.

A married couple from Toronto had no need of the shabby togs pulled from the bottom of warehouse bins, for they'd bought new tailored uniforms in Tel Aviv. Frank had to admit they looked sharp strolling along like Captain and Mrs. Midnight, but he wondered if it was just as easy for terrorists to procure the ensemble.

Even husbands and wives had to live in separate barracks. Frank wasn't the only one who felt claustrophobic in the cramped living spaces. Once when he was taking a break in the common room, the door opened and an American woman entered. "Those rooms are so small, you can't even masturbate!" she announced. He pretended not to hear her.

Another Jewish woman took an interest in Bruce -- a tall, blond man from one of the western states. She was disappointed to learn that he was a polygynous Mormon with three wives and a multitude of kids. One morning after breakfast, Frank happened to be sitting next to him on a bench outside the barracks.

"Bruce, what's this plural marriage thing like?"

"Well, you've got to be living right. If you're not living right, the women won't have you."

Disappointed by this lack of detail, Frank didn't press Bruce for a definition of "living right."

The South African volunteers intrigued him most. The young men all were veterans of the Angolan wars. One had a Jewish father. "Good boys," Frank thought. Somehow, their presence was affirming.

One, however, was clearly crazy. Allen (which sounded to Frank like Ellen when pronounced with a South African accent) never went home, but kept extending his tours. Maybe he had no home to return to. Maybe he had alienated friends and family. He was jumpy, defensive, and – it seemed to Frank -- a little paranoid. A few of the women complained that Allen exhibited misogynistic behavior when they were alone with him in the warehouses. But because he had been there longer than anyone, Allen knew the routine and functioned as camp cadre.

Two women from Cape Town had made the trip together, and Frank found them alluring both individually and as a pair. Zyla was a very pretty blue-eyed brunette. Frank at first took her to be Jewish, but she was a Christian steeped in Biblical mysticism who knew a few words of Hebrew. Hedwig was older and austere, but slender and attractive. A silver pageboy framed her patrician features. She had grown up in Southwest Africa, so she spoke German as well as English and Afrikaans. Frank got Hedwig to banter a bit *auf Deutsch,* and he much preferred her relaxed, euphonic intonation to the overbearing and insistent utterances of many Germans.

On some evenings after supper, Frank and Zyla would sit and talk at the picnic table set up for the volunteers in the barracks square. She told him of her life in tones so soft Frank had to lean in to hear. She was divorced and had a grown son. Frank, too, shared some of his story. He loved her accent and was mesmerized by her voice. Although he was strongly drawn to her, he doubted they would have had a future even if she lived down the block, never mind Cape Town. He believed in God, but Zyla always was finding hidden meanings in scripture, numbers, names, and even common words. She was deadly serious about these divinations, and Frank wouldn't have been able to handle a steady diet of gematria and occult imaginings.

Still, when the volunteers had free time off-post, Frank enjoyed spending it with the two women. Sometimes the army would take the group by bus on sightseeing trips. On a hill overlooking the sea in Jaffa, Frank ached to tell Zyla how lovely she looked, but he didn't want the others to understand. He knew a few words of Dutch and struggled to remember how to say "very pretty" in that language.

*"Heel mooi,"* he said to Zyla.

She looked confused. Were Dutch and Afrikaans that different?

"He means you," Hedwig said.

Zyla thought Frank might have been talking about the scenery. She gave him a shy smile of thanks.

One day after lunch Frank popped his head into another barrack looking for Rob, one of the South African men. The room was empty, but oh my God! There, above Rob's bunk, was a small Confederate flag a volunteer from Texas had given him. The symbolism was stark; the anti-Semites would have loved it. A Confederate banner above the bed of a white South African in Israel. Two lost causes so far. Dear God, he prayed, please don't let Israel be the third.

# CHAPTER FORTY SEVEN

Frank hadn't seen Dahlia in almost two years, and his initial elation had faded in the interval. Reality had overshadowed his romantic daydreams. He and Dahlia lived on different continents almost 6,000 miles apart. She was Jewish; he wasn't. It was hard enough to support himself in Washington. Who would hire a 58-year-old Gentile with no Hebrew in a place where Russian physicists were janitors and concert violinists guarded mall entrances? He'd be lucky if he ended up sweeping the streets.

For her part, Dahlia wasn't going to leave Israel while Gil was still in the army, and soon Nurit would be ready for her two-year term of service. Nevertheless, Dahlia had lived in the United States before. Maybe she'd be willing to do it again. And there always were tourist visas.

Misgivings aside, Frank felt lucky to be friendly with Dahlia and her children. They were a source of human connection in a foreign land. During his first week at Tel HaShomer, imbued with a sense of gratitude and good fortune, he called Dahlia from the pay phone on the edge of the barracks square.

On Thursday, the volunteers lined up outside the chow hall for the midday meal.

"What are your weekend plans?" Martin asked his companions. The army insisted that the volunteers be away from the post on Friday and Saturday. Most took off on Thursday evening and returned to work Sunday morning.

"Linda and I are going to Jerusalem," Davida said.

"I have relatives in Tel Aviv," said Harriet.

"Someone I know has parents in Herzliya," Frank said. "I'm staying with them."

After work the volunteers burst out of the barracks with the enthusiasm of teenagers. Wearing civilian clothes and carrying overnight bags, they began the long walk to the main gate.

Outside the gate, in high spirits, the new friends bargained with taxi drivers for group rates. A gang of five set out for Jerusalem, and Frank hopped into a cab filled with people going to Tel Aviv. He was squashed in the back with his knees against his chest, but a smile was on his face.

Frank got out on Dizengoff Street near the square. He went to a juice stand and ordered fresh squeezed pomegranate. He scrutinized the sign over a falafel shop and took a seat at an outdoor table. Then he checked the time and watched the street.

Twenty minutes later, Frank's juice glass was empty.

A car pulled up driven by an older man.

"Are you Frank?" asked the woman in the passenger seat.

"Yes!"

Frank grabbed his overnight bag and hurried to the car.

"I'm Miriam. This is my husband, Yitzhak Adler."

Frank smiled. He skirted the car to reach the driver's side window and extended his hand.

"Hello!" Frank said to the man. "How are you?"

"Good, good. Get in."

Frank climbed into the back seat.

"Have you eaten?" Miriam asked.

"No, not yet."

"We'll stop somewhere on the way."

"It's awfully nice of you to have me."

"We're happy to do it," the woman said. "We do it for strangers. And you're a friend of Dahlia's."

"Well, we've met only once. But it feels like we're friends. And you have wonderful grandchildren."

"Thank God."

"Your English is very good."

"I was born in Jerusalem during the British Mandate. Yitzhak is from Hungary."

"I came here when I was 16," Yitzhak said, "after the war, around the British blockade."

They stopped at a restaurant where the only conspicuous Jew was an elderly guard at the door. The owners, staff, and most of patrons seemed to be Arabs. The food was good, and Yitzhak rebuffed Frank's offer to pay.

The Adler's home was modest but comfortable.

"You'll be staying in here," said Miriam, leading Frank to the guest bedroom.

"You can leave your bag," Miriam said. "Come sit with us in the front."

Frank set his bag on the floor and joined the Adlers in the living room.

"It's wonderful being here," Frank said. "I'd forgotten what army living was like."

"Tomorrow I'll show you around," said Yitzhak.

"Are you retired?"

"Yes. Agricultural and garden seeds. Did Dahlia tell you that her brother and sister and their families will be here for Shabbat?"

"No."

"And Gil's bringing a friend," said Yitzhak.

"I think the young man has a crush on Nurit," said Miriam.

"What young man wouldn't?" asked Frank.

# CHAPTER FORTY EIGHT

"This is one of my favorite places," Yitzhak said to Frank the next day.

Four shades of blue stretched below them in a breathtaking panorama. White breakers rolled atop turquoise billows along the shore. Beyond the waves, a shimmering ribbon of cerulean bordered an expanse of the deepest amethyst till the sea met an azure sky.

Behind them, a busload of Arab worshippers arrived at the Sidna Ali Mosque for Friday prayers. Yitzhak and Frank watched them disembark. Some were in traditional garb, and some wore Western clothing. A few cast hostile glances at the two infidels on the hilltop, but the Mediterranean had reclaimed their attention.

"It's beautiful, isn't it?"

A well-dressed Arab man of about 25 looked wistfully out to sea. Why did he choose to address us in English? Frank wondered. Do I have "American" written all over me?

"Yes, it's beautiful," Frank said.

"Didn't you come with the others to pray?" asked Yitzhak.

"I know what the old fool will say. He is from the old school and preaches moderation. Fortunately, his time is past."

"You don't think moderation is a good idea for Israeli Arabs?" Frank asked.

"We are one with the Arab nation," the young man said. "You are no different. You believe the Jews of Los Angeles are part of your nation. And what has moderation ever done for us? You are still here after more than 50 years. The time for action has come."

"Action?" Frank said, taking a step toward the Arab. Yitzhak put a hand on Frank's arm to guide him back. "What kind of action?"

"Our young people are blowing themselves up in all your major towns, taking hundreds of Jews with them. President Arafat has promised you a million shahids marching on Jerusalem. Until now you had the upper hand, but your atomic bombs, and tanks, and airplanes won't help you against our martyrs. We've found your weakness. Enjoy the view while you can. "

Frank hadn't been in a real fight in a long time, but he was ready for one now. He would block this boy's punch, and then Frank would go for the eyes, the knee, the groin, the windpipe.

"You're a student?" Yitzhak asked, attempting to defuse the situation.

"Political science, Hebrew University."

Frank spoke softly about a foot from the young man's face.

"I don't think you'll be blowing yourself up anytime soon," Frank said. "I've seen your kind before. You're a talker, not a fighter."

"Here you are," Yitzhak said, still trying to avoid a brawl, "studying at the Hebrew University in Jerusalem, speaking openly of subversion and treason against the State of Israel, without any fear of being arrested, let alone being killed for it. Doesn't that say something to you?"

"Yes. It says that you are weak and that weakness will be your undoing."

# CHAPTER FORTY NINE

On Friday evening, the Adler family gathered around the table for the Sabbath meal. Frank basked in the warm and welcoming atmosphere. He was pleased by Dahlia's attentiveness, and he tried to return her attention without flirting too openly in front of her family.

"More chicken, Frank?" Dahlia asked.

"Just a little piece."

Gil's friend Avi, clearly smitten by Nurit, also tried not to be too obvious about it. Yitzhak and Miriam Adler watched both couples knowingly.

"My Dad's remarried and has a little boy," Nurit said to Avi. "He's so cute! I'm going to see him tomorrow."

"That's in Jerusalem, no?"

"Yes."

"I'm going to be there too. Do you want to get together?"

"Sure. Why not?"

"Let's meet at the Moment Café at about eight."

Dahlia spoke sharply to her daughter. "I told you to stay out of public places, especially in Jerusalem. It's too dangerous!"

"Moth-ther," Nurit said. "Don't worry. This is only meters from the prime minister's residence. It's safe."

⇒╪ ╪⇐

Frank and Dahlia walked on the beach after dinner.

"How did you get to be such a strong supporter of Israel?" she asked. "Are you an Evangelical Christian?"

"No. My background is Catholic."

"Are you still Catholic?"

"Let's put it this way: Jesus of Nazareth believed the God of Israel is the Lord of Creation and the Father of us all, and so do I."

"You seem to be at home with Jews. Did you have Jewish friends when you were growing up?"

"Some." He paused to reflect on his early life. "You know, my father was a man of few words. In fact, he hardly said anything. So when he spoke, you listened. One time he told me about when he was in high school in the inner city during the Depression. He said the Jewish boys were just as poor as he was, but they all had plans. None of the Italian boys had plans. He figured if the Jewish boys could have plans, so could he."

"So what was his plan?"

"He got a scholarship to Cornell, worked part time while he studied, and went on to medical school. The Arabs, instead of blaming Jews for their problems, should follow his example. If the Jews can build a thriving country, the Arabs can too."

"Sometimes I think the world won't like us no matter what we do."

"Western elites approve of Jews only as exiles or victims. They *love* dead Jews! Nazi art thefts are still a big deal. If a painting – a painting! – looted in 1936 is recovered, this is front-page news. 'Never again! Man's inhumanity to man!' But an Israeli mother who has to put her kid on a bus? They don't give a damn."

They walked a few steps in silence.

"Did you like living in the United States?" Frank asked.

"Yes. It was fun living with my sister in New Jersey. They have a big house. And I miss my nieces and nephews."

"Do you think you might like living in the States again some day?"

"Yes. Maybe when Gil is out of the army."

They walked on for a short distance. Frank turned to Dahlia and extended his hand. She took it. They walked under the stars listening to the breaking waves and exchanged shy kisses.

# CHAPTER FIFTY

After sundown on Saturday, Jerusalem came to life. The streets, desolate during daylight, bustled with activity. Buses resumed their service, rolling along with passengers primed with anticipation. And inside the Moment Café, a crowd of young people was having a good time.

On Aza Street, the bomber approached furtively. He entered the café unnoticed but for Nurit. Their eyes locked.

In Herzliya Dahlia and Miriam cleared the dinner dishes while Yitzhak spoke to Frank in German in the living room. The phone rang, and Miriam answered.

*"Ken?"*

Miriam shrieked and slumped. Dahlia grabbed the phone and spoke in Hebrew. She let out a keening sound, her face wracked in anguish. The men rushed over.

On the road to Jerusalem, Dahlia sobbed in the back seat, her mother's arms tightly around her. Frank drove, and Yitzhak gave directions from the passenger seat.

*"Hier links. Jetz, gerade aus."*

Hospital staff scurried to treat the many casualties. Frantic family members tried to learn the condition of victims. Gil arrived in the waiting room, pain on his face and fear in his eyes. Double doors swung open, and a doctor appeared in surgical scrubs.

"Adler?"

Dahlia, Gil, Yitzhak and Miriam rushed over with Frank close behind.

*"Ha im ata ha av?"* the surgeon asked an uncomprehending Frank.

"No, he's not the father," Dahlia said in English.

"The family can go in with her," the doctor said, indicating a nurse.

He shook his head "no" to Frank. "She's very badly wounded. Barely alive." He turned and pushed through the double doors, leaving Frank outside the ward.

Beyond Frank's vision, the family clustered around Nurit's bed. She was swathed in bandages, with needles in her veins and tubes in her nose.

After a short time, the doctor reappeared. "I'm sorry," he said to Frank.

The women reentered the waiting room, broken down in sobs. Gil threw his arms over his head. Yitzhak and Frank looked numb.

The next day Nurit's body, wrapped in simple canvas, was returned to the earth. The large number of mourners surprised Frank. He tried to stay focused during the droning of prayers and the eulogies he couldn't understand.

After the funeral, Frank sat shiva with the family in Herzliya. For the first time, he felt like an outsider. Nurit's father and his second wife were among the mourners, carrying their baby son. In his grief, the man eyed Frank with barely concealed suspicion.

Back in the warehouse, Frank went about his assigned tasks in a daze.

"That's the way it is in this country," said Harriet. "Israel is so small, almost everybody has lost someone to war or terror."

Frank nodded sadly.

"Last week Anna lost a friend in a bus bombing," Harriet said. "She didn't want anyone to know."

Frank stared into a tray of hemostats. He couldn't concentrate, but enjoined himself to carry on. It's the Israeli way, he reminded himself. Hours after some explosions, you'd never know a terror attack had taken place. Israel's message to the world was not "see how we suffer," but rather "we can deal with anything."

But grief is personal, not political. He closed his eyes, and for a moment he saw Nurit's face. Why that precious girl? The religion editor at Consolidated Press had taught him a new word – theodicy -- something to do with why a just and omnipotent God would allow the innocent to suffer and the wicked to prosper. Of course, the word itself explained nothing. Even so, having a name for a terrifying mystery was strangely reassuring. Theodicy was like that last line of movie dialogue. "Forget it, Jake. It's Chinatown." It's theodicy, Frank thought. Don't try to figure it out.

A sentence from the New Testament rattled around in his brain. Was in one of the synoptic gospels? He thought it might be Luke. Yes, Luke had attributed it to Jesus as they marched the Nazarene out to be killed. Frank couldn't remember the passage exactly, so he recast it in his own words: "If this is what they do with the green wood, what will they do with the dry?" Nurit, like Yeshua bar Yosef, had been green wood indeed.

A volunteer worked a push-broom down the aisle in vigorous little thrusts. Frank sneezed from the agitated dust, and he saw Nurit again during the instant his eyes were closed. The whole world was Chinatown, he decided. "Forget it, Frank," he told himself. "It's theodicy."

# CHAPTER FIFTY ONE

In Shin Bet headquarters, Dahlia sat across the desk from an internal security officer, who showed her photos of the suicide bomber taken by the café's surveillance camera. Then he showed her a picture of two distant figures. In a succession of images, the figures grew larger and more distinct. In the final shot, it became clear that the suicide bomber was standing with Ahmed Asfour.

Eyes wide in horror, Dahlia dug her fingernails into her face.

⇥ ⇤

As Frank sat with other volunteers at the picnic table in the barracks square, a phone rang in the distance.

"Frank," said a young man from Manchester, England, "some Israeli person on the line for you."

"Oh, thanks," said Frank. He got up and went to the kiosk at the edge of the square.

"Hello."

"Frank, it's me," Dahlia said.

His face brightened with relief.

"I'm so happy to hear from you! I think about you all the time, but now I feel like an interloper with you and your family."

"You shouldn't feel that way. I'd like to see you."

"You would? How about dinner Wednesday night?"

"I don't feel like going to a restaurant yet."

"No. Of course."

"I'll fix something. Come over about six. You have the address, right?"

"Yes. See you then."

⇒⊹ ⊹⇐

Frank picked up dinner dishes and carried them to the sink.

"Don't bother with that," Dahlia said. "I'll do it later."

Frank rejoined Dahlia at the table.

"There's something I want to tell you," she said, "in confidence."

"Yes?" said Frank, suddenly alert.

"I need to tell someone, but I don't know who. Somehow I believe I can trust you."

"Thank you."

Dahlia was silent for a moment.

"You know that work I was doing for the army? On the psychology of the recruiters of the suicide bombers?"

"You told me, yes."

"I didn't tell you that the government asked me to recommend the release of one of them as a show of good faith. 'No one with blood on his hands,' they said." Her voice ascended in an anguish that startled Frank. "As if you can keep your hands clean doing such work!"

"Don't tell me -- "

"The man I released, Ahmed Asfour, recruited the bomber who murdered Nurit and the others."

Dahlia shrieked like a wounded animal. Frank arose, stepped to Dahlia's chair, gently guided her up by the elbows, led her to the sofa, and sat beside her as she wept. He hesitated, then tentatively put his arm around her shoulders, but he felt more like an older brother comforting a grieving sister than a man with his date.

# CHAPTER FIFTY TWO

The weekend approached, and Frank needed a place to stay, so he decided to rent a room at the Notre Dame Pontifical Institute on Paratroopers Street in Jerusalem. The rooms were clean and reasonably priced and the food a welcome break from army chow. The beautiful limestone "Chapel of Our Lady of Peace" was the most sublime place of worship he had ever seen. In this island of serenity, Frank found refuge from the horror and confusion of the past week.

As usual, a maelstrom of competing thoughts and feelings buffeted Frank's psyche. Our Lady of Peace, indeed. The lady in question was a Galilean girl who (the story went) gave birth six miles from where Frank sat, in Bethlehem *of Judea*, now designated by the world as "the Occupied West Bank." He wondered what Miriam of Sepphoris would have thought of gentile efforts to take the Jew out of Judea -- or, for that matter, from east Jerusalem, the ancient capital.

But the chapel was a place of prayer, he reminded himself. And why not? It was as good a place to pray as any. Frank wasn't an atheist. He closed his eyes. "Heavenly Father," he began. He thought of Nurit, and his stomach heaved. He thought of Dahlia, and he slumped in the pew, his neck and shoulder muscles in spasm. "Dear God, please help the whole family," he implored. He gave thanks that Avi was expected to survive, although perhaps with the loss of sight in one eye.

Peace my ass, he thought. With the City of David only a few hundred yards away, he wanted the kind of peace King David would have imposed. He removed a sheet of paper, damp with sweat, from his cargo pocket and unfolded it. Like Guinevere consigning her favor, Zyla had pressed it into his hands before he left the base. "Take this to Jerusalem," she had said in that voice which broke his heart.

Zyla had written out her rendering of a psalm, attributed to David, that she had synthesized from several of her favorite translations. Sweet Zyla! Serene Arthurian enchantress. She had been such a support to him in the past few days. No sylph queen could have been more gracious. Frank had read the page in the van coming up from Tel Hashomer, and he read it again in the chapel.

### Psalm 110

*The oracle of the Lord said to my honored master: "Sit at my right hand until I make your enemies your footstool."*

*The Lord will stretch forth your scepter from Zion, and you will rule in the midst of your enemies. I begot you in holy splendor even before the sun's creation. Princely power, like dew at daybreak, was yours from birth.*

*The Lord has sworn, and he will not retract his oath: "You are a priest forever, according to the order of Melchizedek."*
*The Lord is at your right hand. He will crush kings on the day of his wrath.*
*He will judge the Nations, smashing skulls and heaping up corpses over the wide earth.*
*Drinking from the stream as he goes, the Lord's anointed can hold his head high in victory.*

Frank wondered what Jeff Hirsh would think of King David's kind of Judaism. And he wondered what King David would have thought of Jeff.

Dan Mendelsohn, a Sar El volunteer from Rochester, New York, joined Frank for dinner at Notre Dame. He and several other volunteers had taken rooms in a hotel on King George Street. Many Jews wouldn't have set foot in a Catholic pontifical institute, so Frank was grateful to Dan for his liberality. Dan was smart and funny, and Frank enjoyed his company. Dan was telling amusing stories about working in the family dry cleaning business when Frank heard a familiar voice.

"Dry sherry, please." It was Peter Lyle. Frank excused himself and walked to the table of the British journalist.

"Tell me, Peter. Is the next generation of Palestinian leaders going to be as murderous as this one?"

"Don't be a cynical, bloody bore," Lyle replied. "Some of the men I'm profiling show signs of being quite moderate. More moderate, in fact, than I'd be in the same circumstances."

"And who might they be?"

"Oh, Fariq Tarahowi. Rashid Odeh. Ahmed Asfour."

"Ahmed Asfour!"

"Do you know him? Say, what's your interest in this? And what brings you back to Israel so soon? Are you on another mission for the Mossad?"

"I may have heard of him. The name seemed to ring a bell."

"The Israelis had him in prison. Flimsy charge. He was released two years ago."

"That must be it. Well look, I've got to go. Good luck with your series, Peter."

Lyle's eyes followed Frank suspiciously as he walked back to his table and rejoined Dan.

# CHAPTER FIFTY THREE

They sat in the office of the same internal security officer who had debriefed Dahlia a few days before.

"Your friend has something to tell me?" the man asked Dahlia.

"Yes," she said.

"And, so?"

"Follow the British journalist Peter Lyle," Frank said, "and eventually he will lead you to Ahmed Asfour."

In the hills of Samaria, on the outskirts of a village near Jenin, a car full of Mizrachi Jews tailed Peter Lyle's vehicle at a discreet distance. When Lyle parked, the Israelis pulled over and watched. Lyle got out and approached a dwelling. The four security men, disguised as laborers, exited their car and strolled forward, chatting nonchalantly in Arabic. They saw Lyle knock, and after a pause the door opened a crack. The Israelis picked up their pace. A man stepped out with a smile of welcome. It was Ahmed Asfour.

Lyle and Asfour shook hands. By now the Israelis were close enough to hear. There would be no need for the army to surround the house in a disruptive midnight raid.

"Let me get my notebook and tape recorder," Lyle said. He returned to his car with Asfour a few steps behind.

"Hands up!" an agent ordered in Arabic.

Asfour's smile turned into an expression of rage.

"Stay back!" another agent shouted at Lyle in English.

Asfour went for his gun. The agents cut him down in a hail of bullets.

"Bastards!" Lyle screamed. "Murdering bastards!"

⚔ ⚔

Frank was stacking boxes in the warehouse when Anna approached.

"I got a call from the main gate," she said. "A man there is demanding, in English, to speak to you. Should I tell them to send him away?"

"No. I'll see what he wants."

As Frank left the volunteer area, he saw a soldier getting into his car.

"Going to the main gate?"

"Yeah. Come on."

Frank took deep breaths as they drove along. The soldier stopped when they reached the gate, and Frank got out.

"Thanks very much for the ride."

The car proceeded through the gate as Frank approached the pedestrian entrance. He walked past the sentries to the parking lot outside the post. There he saw Lyle pacing like a caged animal, watched carefully by two armed soldiers. As Frank approached Lyle in his IDF uniform, the Englishman regarded him with cold fury.

"Look at the fucking kike pig! Have you checked your e-mail, Frank? Tom Sheridan has a message for you. You're sacked! And I'll see to it that you never work in this business again."

Lyle spat at Frank, turned and walked to his car.

Frank watched Lyle pull away. He stood for a few moments drawing more deep breaths. Then he turned and pulled his wallet from his fatigue pants. He showed his ID to the guards, reentered the base, and began the long walk back to the warehouse at Matzrap.

# CHAPTER FIFTY FOUR

Frank arrived at the staging area in a taxi. Soldiers in full combat gear clustered in groups outside the base. Others engaged in last-minute preparations, helping each other with their equipment and adjusting their loads. The young men displayed the racial diversity of Jewish Israel: blond Russians, dark-skinned Ethiopians and East Indians, Sephardim and Ashkenazim. He looked around for Dahlia but didn't see her.

"Frank! Over here."

Dahlia stood near her car with Gil and an Israeli man in his 40s who was smoking a cigarette.

"Tamir!" a soldier shouted as Frank approached, and Gil broke off to join his squad. Dahlia closed the distance with Frank, but the man remained in place.

"He has to go," said Dahlia, controlling her fear. "I know that. But what if I lose both -- ?"

"He's a son to be proud of," Frank said. "And a brother to be proud of."

"Yes."

Frank didn't like the way the man was looking at him. Dahlia walked back to her car, whispered something to the man, and squeezed his arm reassuringly. Then she returned to Frank.

"Is he a relative?" Frank asked, already knowing the answer.

"No. We went to school together. Then I got married; he got married. We lost touch. Last year I heard that terrorists had shot up his car in Judea. He wasn't hurt too bad, but they killed his wife. I called, and we had a short talk. Then he called me when he heard about Nurit. Do you understand?"

"I think so," he said. A few seconds passed in silence. "I understand it's time to go home. I wish you every happiness."

At Ben-Gurion Airport, a young security woman grilled Frank at the El Al check-in.

"Did you pack your own bags?"

"Yes."

"Have they been with you the whole time since you packed them?"

"Yes."

"Has anyone asked you to carry anything?"

"No."

"How long have you been in Israel?"

"Three weeks."

"What have you been doing?"

"Sorting medical supplies at Tel Hashomer."

The girl smiled.

"Thank you," she said.

From the airplane window, Frank watched the skyline of Tel Aviv and the coastline of Israel recede into the distance.

# CHAPTER FIFTY FIVE

F rank called from the lobby.
"Tobias Moore."

"Tobias, it's Frank. I'm downstairs. I have to turn in my phone, sign some documents, and pick up a few things. But my elevator key's been disabled."

"I'll send an intern down."

In the newsroom, most of Frank's former colleagues averted their eyes -- Jeff Hirsh's snub was particularly cold -- but some came up, shook his hand, and wished him well. Frank went to what used to be his cubicle and removed the thumbtacks holding photos of Don and Laura. He put the pictures and a few personal items into his briefcase, reflecting that he had much less to pack up than when he had been fired from The Washington Post three years before.

"Frank, I'm sorry it's come to this." It was Moore's voice.

Frank looked up.

"Thanks," he said.

"I would have interceded if I could, but you crossed a line."

"Yes, yes," said Frank, wanting no lectures on the nobility of the journalist's calling and how he had failed to live up to it.

Moore paused for a moment.

"Did I ever tell you that my father served in Palestine after the war?"

"No," Frank said. "I would have remembered that."

"Yes. He had some stories to tell."

"I expect he did."

"Indeed. He was involved in the search for the kidnapped sergeants. Do you remember that case?"

"Yes," Frank said, trying not to squirm. "Rotten business." It was one of several extreme measures taken in the struggle for Jewish independence that were difficult for him to justify.

Frank knew the basic facts. With the defeat of the Nazis, the Jews of Palestine – then called "Palestinians" – faced two challenges: getting the British out and preparing for the Arab attempt to strangle the new country in its cradle. Haganah, the pre-state army led by future Prime Minister David Ben Gurion, engaged in low-intensity violence against the British but concentrated on smuggling in Jews from Europe and pre-paring for the expected Arab onslaught. Irgun, a much small-er group led by future Prime Minister Menachem Begin -- as well as the even smaller Lehi – waged open war against the British that included unabashed acts of terrorism.

When the British sentenced captured Irgun fighters to death, the group took British hostages whom it threatened to execute if the sentences were carried out. This tactic had some success, but eventually the British sentenced more Irgun men to be hanged. Irgun kidnapped the two sergeants to forestall this, but this time the threat didn't work. Three condemned Irgun men were hanged.

"Did you know they were sergeants in the Intelligence Corps?" Moore asked.

"No, I didn't."

"And did you know that they had been feeding classified information to the Jewish underground – not the lot that killed them, but the main one."

"The Haganah?" asked Frank, with growing astonishment.

"Right. That's why they were so easy to snag. The killers captured them as they came from a meeting with a Haganah operative."

"I had no idea," Frank said, slowly absorbing the sickening implications.

"Yes. I wrote a paper about this at Cambridge. After seventeen days in a tiny concrete cube, the sergeants were strangled and hung from trees. Oh, how they must have pleaded for their lives: 'But we're pro-Jewish! We've risked everything to help your cause – court martial, prison, disgrace! Haven't we shown our loyalty? Why kill us? You've got the wrong men.'

"Did no good, of course. Begin ordered them murdered regardless. The corpses were booby-trapped – you probably knew that. My father was standing in the eucalyptus grove near the captain who cut the bodies down. They expected explosives, so they rigged a knife to the end of a pole. The first body dropped and set off a mine at the base of the tree. Blew the body apart and wounded the captain in the face and shoulder. Dad was peppered with dirt, but the shrapnel missed him.

"When I asked him about the sergeants, he said they were 'silly sods who caused a lot of bother.' He saw them as dupes who had brought on their own destruction."

Moore paused again, but Frank said nothing. Moore removed a piece of paper from a folder.

"I was going to dig this out of the photo archive, but then I thought – why not just print it off the Internet? Must keep up with the times. The quality's not as good, but it'll do." He handed the paper to Frank.

It was the bodies of the sergeants, still hanging from the trees, their shirts wrapped around their heads.

"They were men a lot like you, Frank: idealistic, innocent, naïve, almost eager to betray the trust that was placed in them, and hungry for the validation of others, especially the Chosen Ones. The Israelis always go on about how Arabs never change, but let me tell you – Zionists never change. Jews care only about themselves and other Jews. The Israelis will chew you up and spit you out. A word to the wise, mate."

Moore turned and walked off.

# CHAPTER FIFTY SIX

Frank sat at his kitchen table trying to catch up on bills that had piled up in his absence. A stack of envelopes was at his left hand, a roll of stamps and a ballpoint pen were at his right, and his checkbook was in front of him.

He opened the top envelope and pulled out the bill, holding the paper at a distance so his middle-aged eyes could better see the amount -- and grimaced. He shook his head, sighed, picked up the pen and started writing a check. The phone rang.

"Hello."

"Hi. Are you leaving for work?" It was his daughter

"Oh, hi. No, I've got time."

"I wanted to catch you. How was your trip?"

"It was good. Glad I went. Did you get your grades?"

"Yup," Laura said. "Did pretty good, I guess."

"That's great! What about Don?"

"That's why I called. He's finished the semester, but he's broke."

Frank said nothing.

"We wondered if you could spare some of that money you would have used to take us to Israel. I'm OK, actually. It's more for him."

"Oh, gee," Frank said. "Things have changed. The trip cost more than I expected. Not that much more, but more. And if you had come, I would have had to put some of it on credit card."

"I don't understand," Laura said. "You would have borrowed the money to take us to Israel, but you can't come up anything to help us with living expenses?"

"Don wouldn't have been broke," Frank said defensively, "if he hadn't thrown away his scholarship because he felt he was too good to take direction from his coach. And like I said, things have changed."

"In three weeks?"

"I lost my job."

"Why?"

"Well, my boss didn't want me to go."

"But you went anyway?"

"Yes."

"And you dare to criticize Don? Why are you too good to take direction from your boss?"

"It's not quite the sa--"

"It's exactly the same! I suppose you think we should admire you for going to Israel. What if you had gotten blown up over there? Did you expect us to go around saying how noble and selfless our father was? Our mother can't get across the room without her inhaler, and you travel halfway around the world to risk your life for people you don't even know."

"In a way, I do know -- "

"Well, it only cost you your job. Two kids in college. It's so self-indulgent! I would have thought that your first loyalty would be to us. But I guess it never was. You've always done whatever you wanted no matter how it affected us."

Frank felt like he had been kicked in the stomach.

"I'm sorry you feel that way," he said, "but I can see your point of view."

"You can?"

"Yes."

"If you had seen it a month ago, would it have made any difference?"

"No."

"You would have gone anyway?"

"Yes."

"Don's right about you. You *are* a selfish bastard."

"I don't think we should go on talking right now."

"Bye."

Frank, feeling stunned, carefully replaced the handset on the receiver. He glanced out the window and noticed Janet's car pulling up. She emerged with a shopping bag and walked toward his front door. He got up, went to the door, and opened it.

"Oh, I didn't think you'd be home," she said in surprise. "I brought over a few things you'd left at my place." She looked uncomfortable. "A book, some CDs, a razor, comb, shaving cream – stuff."

Frank took the bag from her hand.

"Thanks," he said.

"How did the trip go?"

"Fine. I got fired."

"Was it worth it?"

"Yeah. Yes, it was worth it."

"You've got nothing to complain about, then. Remember what you told me? Real life doesn't have endings? It just goes on? Good luck, Frank."

Janet turned and walked to her car. Frank stood in the doorway and watched her drive off. He felt like sending an e-mail to Zyla in Cape Town, but what good would that do? It was a pretty Spring day, and the dogwoods were in bloom. Maybe he'd go for a walk later along the canal.

The end

# AUTHOR'S NOTE

This is a work of fiction based on actual events. Public figures are identified by name, and their words and actions are represented as accurately as storytelling allows. All other characters are invented, and any resemblance to actual persons, living or dead, is purely coincidental.

A paragraph in Chapter 4 explaining the protagonist's attachment to the State of Israel is adapted from two sentences in Hillel Halkin's "Land Without Regret," an essay written to mark Israel's 60th birthday, which appeared in the National Post of Canada on May 6, 2008. The adaptation is made with Halkin's permission.

In Chapter 4, an Israeli defense intellectual presents the rationale for Israel's embrace of the "Oslo peace process" in the early 1990s. In the Spring of 2000, the writer attended just such a presentation at a Washington think tank. The author's memory of that briefing was refreshed by endnote 54, pages

706-707, of Ambassador Yehuda Avner's memoir, *The Prime Ministers* (2010), in which Avner recounts then-Prime Minister Yitzhak Rabin's presentation of the same rationale to him in the prime minister's Jerusalem office on November 1, 1993.

In Chapter 45 the protagonist visits the home of geo-strategist Fritz Kraemer (1908-2003). Although the author paid such a visit to Kraemer, the chapter should not be read as a verbatim account of that meeting, in which Israel was mentioned only in passing. Kraemer's assessment of the protagonist's character is a novelistic extrapolation from Kraemer's public statements.

The author has benefitted from the published commentary of Evelyn Gordon and that of Moshe Arens, who has been Israel's defense minister, foreign minister and ambassador to the United States.

The confrontation in Chapter 48 is informed by Solly Ganor's "Conversation on the Beach," an Internet posting of December 6, 2002.

B orn into an Italian-American family in Buffalo, New York,
Louis Marano graduated from Canisius College in 1966
and served two tours in Vietnam with the US Navy Seabees.

Marano earned an MS and an MA from SUNY-Buffalo and
lived with the Ojibwa Indians of Canada from 1974 to 1979. He
received a PhD in cultural anthropology from the University
of Florida in 1981.

After two years as an assistant professor at Drake University,
Marano spent twenty-two years in the news business in

Washington, DC, including ten years at The Washington Post. From 2000 to 2005 he was a reporter, columnist, and feature writer for *United Press International.*

As a civilian contractor for the US Army in Iraq, Marano was a field anthropologist on a Human Terrain Team in 2007-2008 and in 2009 taught at the Army's counterinsurgency school outside Baghdad. He has three children and three grandchildren.

Made in the USA
Monee, IL
31 August 2020